J.E. PITTMAN

Contents

Part 1: Falling Stars

/01/

They call us Pandora Squad – our hope lies in a little box, now very far away.

Light years.

I don't know where we are. They don't tell us, just point us and shoot. Right now, it's hard to know anything except that my head is so filled with noise, I can't even think.

It's all noise. Noise I can't even hear anymore, only feel.

Concussive blasts greeted us. Rocks falling and sand raining down on my helmet. We'd landed in a rockslide. The repetitive hiss of the enemy, almost a chittering sound, was lost on me as we slid down to the cliff base and into the necrobot spiders' advance.

Who the hell thought those were a good idea?

I used to think the only good spider was a dead spider. Now, not so much. Alive, spiders mostly kept to themselves in their webs, eating bugs and, for the larger variety, the occasional small rodent. These dead husks reanimated by the Avispa's foul machinations were abominations.

I felt sick. We all felt sick. Sick from the pressure waves of the sound we could no longer hear converging on us asynchronously. Sick from the dust of another world sucking into our lungs. Sick from the spin of this too-fast planet.

Jenkins acted on it. Or at least tried, his guts likely emptied on the ride over. Poor kid got thrown into this his first day.

I remembered what that was like, the day I'd opened the box...

I'd been given a card by one of the MPs who'd escorted me from my cell and shoved me in a tiny room.

White. Everything was white. The metal chair that should have been stainless, white. The podium the box had been on, white. The box itself, white. All of it white. All of it ran together.

There weren't even cameras in the room to break up the glaring whiteness with the light-sucking abyss of a lens. That would be a violation. Apparently the ritual must be done in secret.

On the card in my hand were the words I was to say, spelled out phonetically.

Over and over again for three days straight. They'd locked me in, the blank door had no handle and disappeared into the seamlessness of the room. Either I came out changed, or I didn't come out at all. That was the deal offered me. No reprieve for the damned, only penance.

By the third day in the sterile white room, my voice cracked along with my mind. Darkness seeped in the crack, grown wider with every utterance of the incomprehensible syllables until it consumed me.

All around me was now black, the world inverted. I felt myself only as a spark of light in that infinite night, a spark which drew the attention of Osiet Ros.

The darkness rumbled, tall as a thunderhead looming, given voice in a dead tongue now licking my brain. The sounds meant nothing — they could have been words, they could have been farts — yet I felt the pressure build. It built until a bubble burst with a rush; it felt like the gooey bits of my brain leaked from my ears. (Later, I was told it was just blood and not to worry about it, but that still struck me as something to be concerned about.)

"You have come to understand me then, Kellan Blaese," the force in my brain spoke. The words appeared wholly formed in my awareness, echoed by a distant rumble. The text of my name in particular lingered in swirling cerulean motes. "Progress," the thunder in my heart whispered.

Around us, deeper into the abyss, I felt others watching, their eyes burning into me. I turned to see, but the darkness concealed them. They were many.

"Elzerath, Ruler of the Host, so bound by another, has decreed we of the Eshali are to assist you feeble fools who seek our aid," the being known as Osiet Ros said and again, the words appeared. "Such is the way of things."

"Cool," I said. Quite profoundly, I felt, seeing that I spoke in the face of madness. "Help me with what?"

"You know not?" I felt this tickled Osiet in some manner. Ah shit. *That's not good.*

"Look, I was just told to go in the room, say the words, and maybe I'd come out alive," I said. Was I alive? I looked around the not-so-empty abyss, wondering if it was some sort of Purgatory. "Better than the death sentence I was given. So what's the deal?"

"We are to become as one, in essence, for a time." The presence of Osiet Ros enveloped me. "Fear not, for I will make you strong, Kellan Blaese."

Ros delivered, making me stronger and faster. We all were. That part was predictable across the board. Beyond that, each member of our squad had been bestowed a unique gift by our rider. Some more useful than others, but each served a purpose.

I snapped back to the rock we'd wound up on. The massive arc of planetary rings crossed the sky. The sight put me ill at ease.

Time to get to work.

I hauled Jenkins to his feet, head-butting his helmet.

"Snap to, guardian," I screamed in his face. Words likely lost in the chaos, but the intent got through. He wiped his lips of spittle and clarity filled his eyes.

I felt a tap on my shoulder and turned. Another of Pandora Squad, Olly Bostock, shouted in my face, talking with his hands when that didn't work. He'd spotted a spider on the rock face above us.

Great landing spot, guys. Not that it was command's fault. They couldn't exactly control where the damn transits came out, but it sure would be nice if they looked before we leaped.

But I guess that's what we're for.

The door-knocker they sent had gone haywire to boot. Its cluster bombs detonating louder and prouder than anticipated, causing the welcoming avalanche. We probably took some casualties right out the gate. At least it had crippled some of the necrobot spiders, too.

The rest were left to us. Whoever had survived.

The one on the cliff hadn't yet noticed us, focused instead on the malfunctioning ordinance and its pretty light show. Glad I wasn't equipped with standard-issue arms; didn't relish the idea of my weapon blowing off my face.

The necrobot spider flexed its legs, slowly lowering its body down the cliff. Testing carefully for loose rock and unstable footing. It was beginning to descend.

Olly did the same, slowly ascending the slope covered in skree, barrel of his new twelve-phase doom tube leading the way. His giant frame moved gingerly so as not to disturb the rock any further, deftly maneuvering the railgun's massive power bank slung over his back. The big man's grace belied the weight of his burden as he motioned for me to follow. Jenkins kept to the rear.

The spider's shiny black legs probed the face, seeking a decent anchor point for its tensile web. It settled on a protrusion of rock, looping translucent white strands around it with two hind legs.

Olly went left; I went right. He'd bring it down. I'd smash the legs. That was the plan.

It was a good plan, I thought, but the spider didn't get the memo. Instead, it sprung from the cliff out into the air. Olly opened fire, tracking the arc of its leap. The twelve-phase hummed to life and flung steel down the doom tube with a rapid whuffing sound.

The cliff face exploded as the solid chunks slammed into it, debris raining down as it crumbled. We'd need new maps when Olly was done. Usually did.

Where the necrobot spider was supposed to be, it was not. Bastard dodged Olly's shiny presents with the whoosh of a booster mid-jump, taking it clear of the arc of steely death. Tensile thread pulled taught, speeding the spider's descent to land on poor Jenkins.

At least it was quick, the sharp foreleg of the necrobot stabbing clear through his chest. Jenkins looked surprised as his body flailed, stuck on the chitinous leg.

Olly adjusted fire, sweeping at the springy feet, which skittered along the skree toward us. I leapt back, higher up the slope, so as not to get caught in the line of fire. Olly had the only range option, being strong enough to carry the pack his rider had helped design. Likely with Olly in mind. The rest of us weren't quite as burly.

But I was quick and had reach, so when Olly ran dry, I intercepted the necrobot speeding toward him as he began to reload. Two of the legs ended in stubs thanks to Olly's onslaught, but this spider was the size of a tank.

Man, I wish I had a tank. Just driving my gun around, sending necrobots to the grinder. Instead, I had knuckle busters. Electric pistons strapped to my arms designed to slam bolts through the spider's hydraulics and bring them down. Up close work. Messy work. Trigger them when your hand's in the wrong spot and it busts your knuckles, hence the name.

I dodged the first clumsy swipe, rolling to my right. The necrobot listed toward a damaged leg, off balance from the swing. I came up punching as it jumped back, just missing a joint. Damn. I skidded along the skree under the spider's body and down the slope.

The smaller ones could be taken out with one shot to the reservoir, their armor not as thick. Easier to squish. But in these bigger ones, the main fluid stores were too well protected. Had to take out the joints to immobilize.

I pressed toward it, zig-zag ducking the stabs as my footing threatened to betray me again. Jenkins' body had thankfully fallen off a ways back. I think it had been on one of the stubs. One strike slipped by my face as I braced my arm up to guard, redirecting the momentum. I launched a hook to the necrobot's knee, knuckle buster triggering on impact, electric bolt slamming home with a satisfying crunch.

Hot viscous goo sprayed my face, smelling like cat piss and somehow tasting sweet. I spat. Nasty. And jumped back as one side crumpled to the ground.

"Clear," I shouted, signaling Olly to open fire.

The twelve-phase hummed to life, hurling metal from the hopper. The barrage tore into the crippled spider, sending bits of chitinous armor flying, its hydraulic lifeblood gushing into the air.

I closed on the necrobot. It still twitched, but it was no longer a threat. The spider's eight eyes narrowed to slits, focusing on me. I didn't know who or what was on the other end, but I wanted to send a message. I clenched my fist and planted the knuckle buster square in the middle of the spider's head. Its mandibles chittered, squirming in an attempt to bite. I fired.

Whatever tension was left in the giant arachnid's corpse released as the brain splattered. The husk collapsed into a heap on the rusty canyon floor.

"You're doing it again," Olly said as I cleaned the ichor from the bolt. He'd walked up behind me, twelve-phase casually resting on his shoulder. Behind him, the hopper's magnetic tail swept the ground for ammo. The design was brilliant, picking up the steel slugs he'd already fired along with any other sort of ferrous chaff.

I didn't have to ask what he meant. Osiet Ros got off on the adrenaline rush. Total battle maniac, Ros, and it tends to show up on my face. I could only imagine the manic look I wore, frenzied bloodlust filling my eyes. Rictus grin, all smeared with purple goo.

A throaty laugh deep inside said it all. Osiet Ros was well pleased.

My cheeks hurt something fierce from the smile that had likely been plastered on my face since I'd headbutted Jenkins at the start of all this.

Jenkins. Poor kid. I walked to what was left of the new recruit.

"Whatever he was guilty of, he didn't deserve this," Olly said, cleaning out his ears.

"None of us do," I said. Pandora Squad was chosen from the vilest ranks of criminals the military could muster. Murderers. Thieves. Traitors. Guilty or not, the accused became fodder for the Eshali.

"He was alive, I think." Olly squeezed his eyes shut. "Trying to get free."

Ah. That's why Olly focused fire on that particular leg. It was hard, I knew. I had some experience in mercy killings.

"He was already dead, Olly," I told him. "He just hadn't caught up to that fact yet." I had my suspicions about that.

Rocks skittered down the slope. We whipped around, Olly taking aim with the doom tube. I charged a bolt.

Luna stopped short, hands raised. Short and quick with a smile, the most easygoing guy in a squad of hardasses. Vicious though. He was Pandora

Squad's sapper, and the traps he laid were particularly terrifying.

"Damnit, Javier." The hopper spun down as Olly lowered the railgun's barrel.

"Ay, Dios Mio," Luna's eyes traveled down to Jenkins. He shut his eyes and made the sign of the cross, saying a little prayer.

"There's no god here," I grumbled. Olly lowered his eyes.

Luna kissed his knuckle and turned to me.

"We march with flights of angels guarding our way," he said. "How can you say there is no God? We are proof of the Divine!" Luna was a devout convert after his time with the box.

Whatever his rider had been filling his head with, I knew for certain my own was no angel. My spine chilled at the thought.

"Angels. Demons. Genies. Aliens?" Olly said, his voice far away. "Lulu says there are many names for the Eshali and the forms they take..."

Olly's rider was the smart one: the professor. Loudain, Olly said his name was. If it was a he. Olly said he, but who knows with the riders.

I couldn't tell if Osiet Ros was man, woman, or something in between. Discomforting is all I knew for certain. The voice in my head, if you could call it that — rarely speaking, only laughing — was pleasantly warm and husky. Deep for a woman or high for a guy, an edge of deceit to it all. Ros laughed at my pontification. My rider seemed eternally amused by my confusion and was loath to volunteer any clarification.

"So they're hackers," I said, half hearing Olly try to explain the quantum metaphysics Lulu fed into his brain. "They jack into our brains from wherever they live and watch and meddle with our shit."

Olly thought about it for a second. Probably asking Lulu.

"That's about it," he nodded. "Simple," Olly added. "I like it. Why can't you explain things more plainly, Lulu?" I didn't know how talkative Lulu was; hard to imagine since Ros hadn't said three words to me since promising to make me strong.

"Blasphemers," Luna shook his head. "Lord forgive these sinners their trespass and lacking faith." He crossed himself again, raising his eyes to an empty heaven.

"I've been called worse," Olly laughed, good-hearted as he was. "Glad to see you made it, brother."

"Major sent me to find survivors," Luna said. "Mi amigo, you make too much noise. Easy," he smiled.

"Ames made it? Damn." Further proof there was no god.

"Been trying to raise you on the radio," Luna said, ignoring my comment.

"Guess the radio got crushed in the slide," I said, shrugging. My pack was gone. I hadn't really noticed during the battle. Didn't care to either. That zealot could shove it.

Luna's faith was admirable, but Ames' fanaticism was dangerous. He'd sacrifice everyone under his command to his perceived greater good.

"C'mon," Luna cocked his head, walking toward the cliff face. "Rossi twins spotted a nest."

The transits aren't super stable, dumping us out on the slide while the rest of the unit had apparently landed on the other side of the prominence. I'd seen men sliced in half stepping through at the wrong time. Piss poor luck there.

Did any of us have good luck, though?

"Major's set up a kill box on the other side of this rock," Luna said. "Dug the twins in to run their drones, set up the less *portable* railguns," he said, looking at Olly's concoction.

"Works real well," Olly patted his anisotropic twelve-phase doom tube.

"Sure does," I added. "Good idea, Lulu had."

"I asked him for it," Olly grinned. "I figured as long as I was carrying a nuke, I should use it to run something useful."

Olly's pack did function as a nuke. Overload it, go boom. Last option should things get out of hand.

"Olly," I'd been wondering something, "when Lulu talks to you, do you understand him?"

"Well, yeah," Olly puzzled over the question. "I mean, sometimes he uses too many big words, but yeah. Why?" he raised his eyebrow.

"Osiet just rumbles at me, and the words show up in my head," I explained. "Wouldn't understand a damn bit of it without the subtitles."

"Hunh," he scratched his head. "I guess Lulu rumbles, too, now that you mention it. But then he gets dubbed." Olly smiled and added, "Doesn't sound anything like the rumbling."

"Dubs never do," I laughed.

"Careful where you step here," Luna broke in, slowing pace. "Don't want to trigger the surprises."

I stopped and looked around. I saw nothing, but that was the point. Luna's rider let him bind things. Like bombs to rocks. Pit traps made of solid ground until the wrong thing walked over it. Flip side of his power let him dismantle things, too, violently.

I didn't know who had what, above my pay grade, but I knew some of what we could do. Olly was pretty obvious. I'd heard one guy could walk on water. Doc could heal some injuries, and our cook could multiply rations. That was pretty handy. It was a total mixed bag, some more useful than others. Practical and tactical.

Always in balance. Mine encouraged fruit and vegetables to bountiful harvest. I actually liked that side of my gift, but not terribly useful on a desolate rock like this. The counterbalance to that struck me as being off by an order of magnitude, though, and I'd be damned if I used it. So, I stuck to my knuckle busters.

Periodically, during our careful march through the sapper's minefield, he knelt behind us and scratched marks into a ceramic tile. He muttered the dead language we all seemed to hear in our brains, no longer needing the phonetics. Trap set, he covered the tiles with dirt, closing the holes he'd left in his perimeter for our passage.

We carefully approached the railgun placements, announcing our approach to friendlies. Their long barrels swung our direction, taking sight. Imposing, sure, but Olly's twelve-phase doom tube was a vast improvement on these long guns. Drones buzzed overhead, identifying us. I flipped them off, knowing the major would be watching.

Olly wasn't the only one who changed maps, I noticed. One side of the canyon had been brought down to create a funnel for the railguns to fire into. The necrobot spiders' ability to parkour the shit out of these cliff walls was troublesome, to say the least. This was about the only thing we could do about it. I felt sure the other canyon wall was rigged to blow should eight legs be set upon it. One of Luna's traps.

"Lister, Ellis," I nodded to one, then the other manning the pinch point behind the gunners buried in their bunkers. Each held a vicious-looking hammer mounted to a long pole. Nozzles protruded from the backs of the impact drivers. Useful for busting some kneecaps, boosters giving them a little extra kick on the follow-through. Tomahawks hung from their belts in case the spiders got too close. Wide-bladed, curving to wicked spikes on the back.

"Blaese," they nodded coolly. No doubt wishing I hadn't survived. Can't blame them. I didn't have the best reputation. The major'd seen to that.

"Be nice, boys," Olly smiled at them. "He's saved all our asses more than enough." My only ally in this unit of the forsaken. Probably for the best. Getting along with murderers galled me. These two, especially, liked killing.

"Where's Jenkins, then?" Ellis sneered in response.

/02/

Olly's face darkened. Shame and guilt mixed with his protective nature. No doubt what happened to the boy ate at him deep inside, and these two buffoons had stepped right in it, trying to insult me.

I put my hand on his shoulder, tensed for a strike. Olly shouldn't be here. He wasn't cutthroat like the rest. Gentle to a fault, smothering the temper inside. Victim of shitty luck that when his control lapsed, he'd punched a senator's kid in a bar brawl. The kid fell badly, hitting his head and cracking it open on a curb.

"It's okay, Olly," I whispered to him before stepping forward. "Couldn't save him. Piss poor luck he got spit out on my side of the mountain," was all I said.

"Bostock! Blaese!" The major crawled out from under his rock, wherever he'd been hunkered down with the drone monitors. The two guards stiffened to attention. Luna fell in. I slouched. Olly was Olly again, thank goodness. "Report."

"Guardian Jenkins, killed in action," I said, leaving no doubt about it. "Dozen small enemy units disabled in the landslide. Enemy tanker disabled by Guardian Bostock," I gave Olly the credit.

"And so another sinner has paid his due," the major called out. Back stiff, voice hard. "Jenkins has been delivered to the final judgment of the Lord."

Major Ames paced before the three of us, inspecting his wayward sheep. He turned, addressing the squad gathering around.

He prayed, fevered eyes distant. "May all of us sinners one day be so lucky. Luna," he snapped, stick firmly up his ass.

"Yes, sir," Luna saluted. "Perimeter established and countermeasures set, sir. They get close, they go boom, sir." Luna smiled.

"Good man. Now, you sinners," he called to the entire unit milling about their tasks. "Like Joshua chapter eight, verses seven and eight, ye shall be."

"Care to clarify for us heathens," I snarked. Always with the obscure verses. Just tell us what you want us to do besides die. He walked over to me and stared.

"Why thank you for volunteering, Blaese." The major smiled in my face, too close. "The enemy is on their way, pouring from their nest, no doubt stirred up by your earlier arrival."

"That wasn't our fault," I said. "The door-knocker malfunctioned."

"No excuses," he spat. "Surveillance shows the bulk of their force here." The major drew a rudimentary map in the dirt. "Moving toward our location," he stabbed at the ground. "Leaving their nest sparsely defended."

"Convenient," I muttered.

"Divine provenance from the Lord," Ames countered. "Unworthy as we are, He sees our hand strikes where it withers the enemy. And you, Blaese, shall be as Joshua's spear," the fervor increased. "Lie in ambush outside their nest, and while they assail us, render them unto desolation." His eyes hard as he delivered his condemnation. No one with me could survive that.

Ames turned on heel and strutted before the rest of the unit.

"The rest of you will take incendiary ordinances to this point on the canyon wall," the major stabbed the map once more. "And obliterate anything that comes through the canyon." He was going to get them killed.

"Major," I interrupted. "All ballistic and incendiaries seem to malfunction here, as the door-knocker did." The gathered squad muttered at that revelation.

"Is that so, Blaese," Ames glared. "Guardian," he snapped at the man named Leland, unfortunately in the major's line of sight. "Fire your sidearm."

"Sir?"

"One round, into the air," the major said, his voice conveyed an air of reasonableness at the order. "Fire."

Leland hesitated, looking around for help.

"I said, fire." With a voice like ice, Major Ames uttered words in the dead tongue under his breath, enforcing his will.

I barely made out the name of Leland's rider in the string of syllables, when his eyes went wild, hand moving of its own accord.

"No, stop," Leland cried, taking his service weapon from the holster. "Please," he begged. His arm rose over his head, hand gripping tight. I watched in horror as he squeezed the trigger.

Leland's weapon misfired, as I knew it would. As the major knew it would.

The pistol exploded, mutilating Leland's hand in a cloud of hot metal shrapnel. The burning shards tore at his face and arm as well, one piece lodging in his eye. Leland screamed, face and stub of arm gouting blood.

The unit stood — some terrified, others with empty eyes — watching the broken man crumple into a wailing ball of pain before their eyes.

Olly broke first, coming to the maimed man's aid. Taking Leland's belt, cinching it brutally tight around the stump of his arm to cut off the blood. The cries ceased, the man succumbing to shock. Or to death.

"Thank you, Guardian Blaese," the major said, standing over Leland, "for this vital demonstration. Take him to Lowry," Ames nodded at the body crumpled at his feet.

I grabbed Leland's boots while Olly grabbed his shoulders and hoped Lowry, our medic, could work a miracle. Or a kindness.

The major continued laying out his deranged plan for all the men he'd get killed. I couldn't bear to listen anymore. I'd tried… I'd tried.

We took the wounded man deep into the back of the bunker, finding Doc Lowry examining another patient by the light of a signal flare.

"Doc," Olly called. "Leland's hurt bad."

"Put him there." Lowery waved his flare at a cot, not looking at his new patient. Instead, he spat in the eye of the man he'd been treating and muttered more dead syllables. I often forget how flagrantly most can use the gifts bestowed upon them.

"You could as well." Osiet Ros rumbled, the glowing words formed whole in my awareness once more.

"No," I snapped back. I would not give in. The thunder in my heart laughed.

Olly looked sick.

"How'd he do that, Kellan," he asked plaintively, holding Leland's good hand. "How'd he do that? Lulu won't answer."

"By Elzerath's will," Ros supplied, suddenly chatty. "All who serve unto him do as bid."

"The riders," I said to Olly. "Leland's rider made him do it." Goddamn it.

Explosions went off in the distance, shaking the cave. Luna's traps, at least, benefitted from the extra oomph on this forsaken rock. The spiders were coming. This canyon would soon be crawling with necrobot spiders.

"Go," the doc said. "I've got him." He began muttering again, sprinkling white powder over Leland, yanking the shrapnel from his eye.

"Damn," I cringed. "Go easy on him, Doc."

He shooed us out with a stern look, never breaking the healing chant, calling upon the Eshali.

Outside was a flurry of activity, grunts hopping about the bunker carrying munitions, rounds for the railgun, bolt-bows — designed to sling rods through spider joints. Like my knuckle busters, but long range. Not very accurate either. But better than having a rifle explode in your face.

Each man followed the major's orders without question. Were they simply afraid, or had their riders taken control? Meat puppets dancing on celestial strings, no different than the necrobots? The thought gave me pause. Ros chuckled.

The men formed up at the gate, the major extolling the virtues of sacrifice in the absolution of their sins. Half would ambush the enemy, the rest would ostensibly defend the transit mouth here, and grind the enemy between the gun placements and ambushers. He dismissed them to what would no doubt be their graves. My heart sank; there was no saving them from the fanaticism.

/03/

Three men waited closer to the walls, listening to the major's benediction, waiting for Olly and me.

Luna smiled at our approach, handing me a replacement radio and patting Olly on the back. "Ready for more, hermanazo?"

"No choice but," Olly said, hiding the sadness and confusion he'd been facing. He knew no good would come from it, not right now.

Bridges said nothing. He was stiff, wary of both the major and myself. Smart man, kept his head down. Armed with one of the impact drivers and a belt full of grenades.

Last came one of the Rossi twins. Dustin, I thought. Portable drone launcher strapped to his back, his only weapon a small bolt-bow in one hand. The other hovered near a joystick to control the drones. Eyes covered with glowing goggles I knew gave him an overlay on the world.

"Remember, Blaese," Ames said as Olly and I geared up. "Should you fail to be the spear, Bostock becomes the Pillar of Salt." A none-too-gentle reminder that he'd trigger Olly's nuclear backpack should I decline to bring down judgment upon the target. "I'd hate to lose access to Loudain, but that would only be a temporary setback." We were all replaceable.

I glared, snapping my second knuckle buster in place. Ames smiled. It was an unpleasant smile, all teeth and gums and too small lips.

"Move out," the major ordered.

Our group took the path less traveled, up the back of the canyon wall. Luna had set up a rope ladder while we had seen to Leland, apparently. We were to bypass the oncoming enemy column, circling around and going straight for the control center in the nest.

Rossi launched his drone when we crested the prominence, the glowing goggles brightened as the drone gave him a bird's eye view. "Clear for three clicks," he reported, setting off in the direction his drone had gone.

Inside my head, Osiet Ros grew restless. Eagerly anticipating the coming battle and my hand being forced. I dreaded it. Olly might be the nuclear response, but my *gift* was the Biblical. My Eshali smiled.

The ground shook with violent tremors. Terrain shifted, kicking dust up toward the horizon. The necrobots had made it into the canyon, setting off Luna's biggest trap.

"Guess it's starting now," I said, looking toward Rossi. My radio had remained silent so as not to chance revealing us to the enemy, but I knew he was getting a live feed from his twin. He grimaced, but said nothing.

Olly itched his trigger finger on the guard of the twelve-phase. He'd rather be in the thick of things than sneaking around like a coward. He always felt he could turn the tide, especially when squad mates died. And he could, but there was only one of him, and he was needed another place. He'd get his wish soon enough. We pressed on, descending from the highlands.

There was no cover, flat ground as far as the eye could see. We'd be spotted in an instant out here. I didn't like it. I didn't like it at all. We kept going, heads on a swivel. Olly kept the hopper spinning, sweeping up more ammo, just in case the spiders had an ambush of their own. I charged my bolts.

Rossi vanished with a splash. Nowhere to be seen.

"Rossi!" Olly and I got back to back, Luna with Bridges. We swept the horizon. "Anybody got eyes on him?"

We heard the drone buzz overhead, homing in on its operator. "That way," Luna pointed.

One area of dusty, flat land looked exactly like the next, the drone hovering over one spot. Rossi was nowhere to be seen. We closed on the spot, and the grainy ground rippled, rolling upon itself with a splash.

"Shit." I got down to the ground, quickly edging closer to where Rossi had gone under. "No one said anything about quicksand." He'd been under for minutes at this point.

I took a breath and plunged forward into the abyss. There was no light in the blackwater, all of it blocked by the floating sand. It was thinner than I expected, throwing me off balance as I slipped further from the edge. Only death awaited.

I felt a firm hand grasp my ankle and start hauling me back.

I caught a glimpse of wan yellow light, the glow of goggles, drifting far down below. It didn't move. From even further below came veins of malevolent orange glow, waiting to consume our fallen comrade.

I gasped for air, breaking the surface. Once more in the blessed light. Grit filled my mouth as I struggled to breathe.

"Kellan," Olly smacked me. "Kellan," he said again, shaking me. I coughed.

"Easy, easy," I said, blinking away the grit. I coughed again. "You know how when we were kids, TV shows had us convinced quicksand would be a huge problem, and then it wasn't?" I spat out more grit.

"Yeah?"

"Well it is again," I said, looking out over the deceptively calm flatness. There was no way to tell how far it went by looking at it, or if there was even solid land to be found on the other side.

Luna knelt by the edge, scooping his hand through the watery muck. He said a silent prayer for Rossi and again made the sign of the cross.

"Lulu says it's pumice," Olly shared, reluctance in his voice. "Volcano rock. Full of bubbles, so it floats," he said. I didn't think he and Lulu had spoken much since Leland. "Rocks shouldn't float," Olly added. "Ain't natural." He launched a few rounds out over the concealed blackwater.

Whufwhufwhuf. Splash. Splash. Splash.

Another burst, another direction.

Whufwhufwhuf. Splash. Splash. Crack. The last round skittered across solid ground.

"Pretty fur bit there," I whistled. Had to be a hundred feet, maybe more. Olly's twelve-phase didn't have *that* long a range.

"Bridges, you're up," Luna said.

"You're swimming him across?" I asked, confused. Full gear, he'd never make it.

"No." Bridges pulled out a hunk of lead inscribed with Eshali and began chanting, his eyes closed. The glyphs began to glow cerulean; motes of light danced about his feet.

"Why'd you think I brought the cook along?" Luna laughed. "In case we got hungry? Link up!" Practical and tactical. A gift for each.

Luna put his hand on Bridges' shoulder, I put mine on his, Olly bringing up the rear. My stomach somersaulted, always nervous when we defied physics.

Weapon in one hand, tablet in the other, eyes still closed, Bridges stepped out onto the concealed blackwater and did not sink. Two more steps, and Luna was walking on the water. Another two and I stepped onto the rippling surface. It didn't give way, but it felt like it could at any second.

Chanting the entire way, Bridges walked us across the abyss, never once opening his eyes.

Somehow, the stone-covered water was even able to take the weight of Olly and his reactor. Solid ground could barely manage that.

And then it didn't. I felt the hand on my shoulder let go as Olly sank with a splash beneath the blackwater that now undulated angrily beneath our feet.

"Olly!" I turned to grab for my friend.

"Damnit, Blaese, don't let go," Luna grabbed my hand so we stayed connected. "Bridges, quick march."

The cook squeezed his eyes shut, chanting harder as we sped up, trying desperately to maintain focus.

We made it to the shore, turning at the edge, hoping Olly was somehow afloat behind us. He was nowhere to be seen.

I rounded on Bridges and grabbed his collar, shouting in his face.

"What happened? Why'd he sink?" Anyone but Olly. He didn't deserve this.

"He's gone, hermano," Luna pulled me off Bridges. "He's gone."

/04/

The surface broke behind us in a violent burst of legs and muck.

"Yee-haw," Olly shouted, riding a damn water spider as it tried to impale him. The amphibious necrobot lashed about, sending spray everywhere.

Luna burst into bright laughter, shouting, "Ride that fucker, gringo!"

I said nothing, just happy to see my friend again. I hadn't realized my heart had stopped until it now beat again.

"Kill it with fire," Bridges shouted.

Olly jammed the barrel of the doom tube in between the snapping mandibles trying to eviscerate him and pulled the trigger, unleashing a point blank barrage of hypersonic steel.

The spider went limp as its head exploded. Violent thrashing replaced with gentle floating.

"Give a fellow a tow!"

Luna tossed him a rope. We braced as Olly took hold of the lifeline, pulling his improvised corpse raft to shore.

"Damn, brother, don't do that," I smacked Olly on the back once he hopped ashore.

"Sorry, just felt like a dip," he grinned. "Been too long since my last bath."

"Give me a hand, lover boys," Luna called. He'd started dragging the necrobot ashore.

"What're you doing?" I asked as I grabbed one leg. Olly took another.

"The Lord has provided, and we'd be fools to waste," Luna said as he plunged a knife into the spider's abdomen, working at a joint in the armor. He muttered some words, and the carapace split, revealing the treasure he sought.

Spools of spider silk. Stronger than steel at a fraction of the weight. These looked fresh, too. The dead could make webs no more, but they could reuse what they'd found and taken up.

Inside the husk was remarkably dry given the mess they made when splatted. Tubes ran everywhere, feeding back to the central reservoir. I'd rarely gotten the chance to look inside the reanimated corpses after I'd killed them again.

And I wouldn't this time, either. The drone that had been idly hovering zipped over to us and circled before heading off to the nest.

Time to move out. We each took lengths of silk, looping them across our chests, and set out. Bridges led the way, probing the ground with the butt of his hammer as he went.

The ground gradually rose again as we made our way among the hills, climbing higher and higher until we came to the foot of a mountain. Strung between it and another, was the necrobot spiders' nest. Clouds of white webbing spun into a vortex at the mouth of a valley. Sacs strung along the mountainside opposite us housed the eggs of generations yet to come.

The surface of the nest crawled with activity. Living spiders tended the young while the necrobots stood guard, keeping them in as much as keeping intruders out. Others of the living gathered webbing like that across our chests to replenish the reanimated husks' supplies. Their legs carefully worked to coil the strands they spun.

I had never seen the spiders before they'd been transformed into cold killing machines. They looked remarkably...normal. Just going about their daily chores. Peaceful, if you didn't see the guards.

"So that's what they look like when they aren't trying to kill us," Olly said. "Not what I was imagining."

"Never is," Luna shook his head. A hint of regret tinged his voice.

"Let's get this over with," Bridges said, skidding down the slope. He tripped their trap.

Out of the ground sprung hundreds of little necrobots. Individually, easy to squash, but in numbers, they overwhelmed. They surged over Bridges' body, covering him in writhing legs as he spun to sling them off. The boosters on his hammer hissed to life, whirling him around as he lay about with the impact driver, trying to clear himself from the swarm.

I started toward Bridges to help the man swat the crawling death, but too late. Their mandibles were making quick work of him. He fell. And in one last act of defiance, pulled the pin from a grenade at his waist.

"Cover!" Luna and Olly hit the ground. I jumped for cover as the chain reaction started. The grenades burst energetically, their incendiaries, enhanced by the planet's atmosphere, catching the swarm alight.

One spider, then another, catching alight in the blaze. Hydraulics boiled in the inferno, husks started popping. Hell-bent on destruction, the burning necrobots swarmed toward us.

Olly opened fire, twelve-phase spinning to life, hurling death downslope at the skittering flames. Mental note: killing it with fire does not always work.

Luna tackled me to the side as one of the big spiders landed where I'd been. We scrabbled away as it brought a sharp leg down to skewer us.

It missed, but turned and swung at Olly, catching the big man in the side as he tried to dodge. Olly slammed into a rock, slumping over.

"You bastard," I cried, charging the necrobot spider. I primed my bolts as I closed in, ducking one strike, dodging another. I swung an uppercut at its thorax, hoping to puncture the trunk line. The bolt drove home, and I double-clutched, striking it again. It stabbed at me with its wicked sharp leg, grazing my back as I dove forward in a roll.

I'd cracked the carapace, barely. Purple fluid seeped from the fracture as it sprang back to higher ground, proverbially licking its wound. It did, however, patch the leak with gobs of webbing as it stared, eight eyes watching me and Luna, now off to the side checking Olly.

"How is he?" I called, squaring off with the necrobot, placing myself between it and my prone friend. I didn't take my eyes off it for a second, not even to see if Olly survived.

"Breathing," Luna confirmed. "Good pulse. He'll be okay." The sapper hauled Olly upright, sitting him against the rock. "Any ideas?" he asked, rejoining me.

"Kill it," I said coldly.

"Simple," he said. "I like it."

Before we could enact my plan, the necrobot vanished, quick as lightning.

Backs together, Luna and I swept the sight lines around us, tensed in readiness for an attack. None came for several minutes.

A whole lot of things about this entire situation bothered me. Time for answers.

"Okay, what are they?" I spoke the question aloud, but knew in my head Osiet Ros had been gleefully watching.

"Hermano?" Luna looked at me with concern.

"The enemy," came a rumbled reply. "That's all you need to know." Distant. Still speaking in subtitles.

"The hell it is," I railed. "I'm tired of this bullshit. Of people I don't know in rooms I don't know exist, deciding my fate when they don't even know my name." Luna nodded along, like me, tired of being a weapon. Osiet Ros filled with wry mirth.

"Then take fate into thine own hand," the Eshali tempted me. Gleeful at the thought.

"Who are they?" I put the question to Ros again. Luna looked on in silence, wanting answers himself.

"Captives," Ros said, gleeful madness put aside for the moment. "Fodder for the war. The Avispa harvest their bodies and turn them into assault weapons.."

"Captives," I repeated aloud. "Bred to die."

"Goddamn it." Olly had come around, his jaw clenched. Whether in pain or outrage, I wasn't sure. Likely both.

"He does indeed," Luna nodded. "We are all of us condemned."

"No," I said with a wry laugh. "Just me."

As if on cue, the buzzing drone returned to gaze down on us with its soulless eye. The radio hissed and crackled.

"Blaese," the major called. "Destroy them now," he ordered. Explosions came through in the background. Men screaming. "Destroy the nest; the rest will fall."

"I won't," I said, defying his order. "I won't do it!" My radio squelched in my white-knuckled grip.

On the other end, men were dying. I had to wonder if they were all as corrupted as the major.

Silence. Then. "Revelations twenty-one, eight."

My head suddenly hurt. Stabbing behind my eyes. Osiet Ros giggled, twisting the knife.

"No," I wailed. On Earth, my gift manifested as a vicious hailstorm sent to rend the soil and strip fruit from its branches.

"But the fearful, and unbelieving, and the abominable," the major began quoting as my arms stretched out of their own volition. Here... my eyes turned up toward the vast rings in the sky.

"and murderers, and whoremongers, and sorcerers, and idolaters," Ames went on. I began the chant that would rain hellfire down upon us all.

"Stop this," I cried in my mind, my mouth still chanting as I felt the storm gathering high up in the heavens, ready to descend on the nest before me.

"and all liars," the major spat, his voice filled with madness.

"No." Osiet Ros was gleeful to finally see the ruination I could truly cause.

"shall have their part in the lake,"

A thought struck, terrible and evil, but necessary. I reached wider, pulling in even more of the orbital debris...

"which burneth," ...which began to ignite in the atmosphere.

Osiet Ros burst with malevolent joy, coming close to climax. Aiding in my slight alteration of the order.

"with fire and brimstone," the major's voice crescendoed as the skies lit with the fires of hell raining down.

"which is the second death," he finished.

My chant done as well, I collapsed in a heap and watched death descend from above. I weakly grasped my radio.

"Revelations twenty, verse ten, bitch."

The first rocks struck the nest, destroying everything alive and dead. The cries of the living spiders as they burned, I will never unhear.

"And the devil that deceived them was cast into the lake of fire and brimstone," Luna recited, scratching at a tile.

"You insolent..." the radio crackled, then cut off.

The sound of distant explosions reached us.

"...where the beast and the false prophet are," Luna crossed himself, gazing up at the heaven falling upon us.

"And shall be tormented day and night forever and ever," I finished.

I couldn't stop the genocide I'd wrought, but I could bring its architects to their judgment.

The mountain crumbled around us.

Part 2: Silken Symphony

/05/

The world'd closed around me, everything turning off except for my nose — wet copper mixed with the dirt I'd been eating, coming through loud and clear. It'd been a while since I smelled blood in my nose, tasted the tang on my tongue — the necrobot spiders tended to be stabby, not punchy.

I liked to punch, though.

Seventy-four fights, in and out of the ring. Seventeen-and-three — with one draw — on base, forty-three-and-six off. One draw off, too, to the same guy — my big brother Gerald.

Well, he might as well have been. Shit kicked around the same foster homes together for ten years. Taught me how to drink, cuss, smoke, and, most importantly, fight. A year and change older, he had a couple inches and a couple dozen pounds on me — which he used to good effect. After following him into the Army, G taught me to survive — through basic, regiment, and two tours — the man had always been there for his little brother.

Now it was my turn.

"Ow, son of a..." I felt the phantoms of all seven-hundred-forty-three punches I'd taken come rushing back. Distantly, thunder rippled with glee.

"Punch *through* your target, Blaese," the sergeant barked at my mistake. "just like boxing." I knew a thing or two about that, but against brutes — not tree trunks.

"Roger, Sarn't Bradford," I shouted, shaking out my gauntleted fist, raising my other for guard. It was the first time I'd actually used a knuckle buster on a moving target, and it hurt like hell. The shockwave from the piston firing numbed my arm to the shoulder. Like the first time I'd racked the slide after a mag change in basic — bit the shit out of my hand — it was the last time I'd make that mistake — what they call self-correcting.

Numb or not, I couldn't stop — not during a stress round. My heart was about to burst after the run, but the targets kept coming. Ten klicks, then scrabble up a scree slope to the box where the test actually began. It was hell, but that's where they were sending us — better get used to it.

I felt ridiculous, like I'd been dumped into a giant claw machine — with me the prize. I rolled, dodging another swiping leg.

When the spiders died — well, again — they seized up, and the Force hadn't figured out how to turn them back on and run the damn things. So, some scientists had the brilliant idea to take the husks and mount them to cranes with hydraulics running down the cable to operate the corpses. They were a little twitchy and clumsy, but better than nothing.

Remind me to send the scientists a nice thank you note, I thought as a second crane-spider swooped in from the left faster than I could deal, knocking me off my feet. The thunder laughed again as the leg swung down on me.

"And you're dead," Sergeant Bradford called, the spider's spearing leg inches from my face. "So are you, Gonzalez, the fuck you think you're doing up there?" he called up to the crane. "How's he supposed to learn if you *kill* him?" He'd come way too close.

"Bostock!" The sergeant called for next as I left the box. Olly'd just finished the run up the scree, barely huffing or puffing. Asshole.

The crane-spiders came to herking life, jerking up into the sky as Olly charged the box, beginning the drill. Not wasting any time, he leapt for the big one as it rose — strength enhanced by his rider, the big man veritably flew into the air, grabbing hold of a twitching leg.

I whistled in appreciation. As yet unburdened by the *insurance policy* they foisted on him later, he could move — and wasn't done yet. One arm wrapped around the stabby-leg he reached up to punch at the joint with the other. Two cracks of his fist were all it took to separate it from the body — no knuckle buster needed for Olly.

Gravity kicked in at that point, Olly falling down to the dusty rock with his prize, bouncing a bit before righting himself in a crouch as the other spider swung in from his blind side, catching him in its grip.

Never get in a hugging contest with Olly Bostock. It won't end well for you, as the spider would have found out — had it still been alive, er, active. Instead, the crane operator — Gonzales had that one, I think — found out as Olly wrenched one arm free and cracked the spider's head with an elbow. At which point he stabbed the remnants of the leg he held through the opening, cutting all the hydraulics.

"Out-standing, Bostock!" Bradford made some marks on a small pad before tucking it away. "But next time, don't get caught." No matter how good you run the course — how perfect the performance — they're always going to find fault. Keeps you on your toes.

"Ro'er, Sarn't." Olly wiped the spewed hydraulics from his face and came to his knee. Dust and grit made a grim mask mixed in the purple fluid turning his grin deathly.

Dirt and rubble clattered around me, my ears coming back as light broke through the darkness, blinding my bleary eyes.

Olly's face again — same rictus smear of grit and blood, his own this time — grim, turning to bright when I coughed.

"Kel!" Olly scooped more rock away from where I lay battered among the rubble of my grand defiance. "He's alive," the big man called down. To whom, I wasn't yet sure. Had Luna made it, too? Damn, I hoped so. He was good people.

Pincing mandibles beneath eight red eyes appeared over Olly's shoulder, bearing down to snip his head clean off. I lunged...

Or tried to, my arms still pinned, my legs wouldn't move.

"Olly," I cried, frantically trying to free myself. "Behind you!"

Blood boiled in my brain as the thunder in my heart readied another strike, unbeckoned. Desperate, I almost relented as the spider's shadow closed on us both — chittering now reaching my ears.

"It's okay, Kel," Olly smiled, disarming death from above. "This is Ciacha," he pointed over his shoulder. "She pulled us out."

"Like the dance?" Confused, I barely processed. Necrobots always went for the kill, and now I was picturing this one — browns and blacks with orangish stripes — doing the eight-legged cha-cha. I must've taken more brain damage than I thought.

"Kill it." Osiet Ros flashed the words before my face in a rumble. "Now, before it dines upon your liquid entrails." Scenes of such horrors flashed — forced — in my mind.

I squeezed my eyes shut, silencing the thunder and stilling my heart.

More chittering, but none of the tell-tale hiss I was accustomed to hearing from the necrobots. Ciacha, Olly had called the spider, rose higher on its massive legs. I saw a crack on the thorax, sealed with webbing but still leaking purple goo. It was the same spider I'd struck before the collapse when Bridges stumbled on the trap.

I knew something had seemed off about it — it was not a reanimated husk. It still lived. Ciacha's eyes blinked in a ripple, shifting from Olly to me as it chittered — angrily? Olly frowned.

"He won't hurt you again if I ask him not to," Olly said, turning his head up to the spider. It seemed to nod. Did it know what the big man said?

"You can understand it?" Olly never ceased to surprise. Due to his size and surprisingly gentle nature, people often mistook him for a dullard and brute — barely two thoughts to rub together in his head. Boy were they wrong. I always thought Loudain picked Olly for his good sense. He might not be book smart, but he had an innate understanding surpassing many. Still waters run deep and all.

"Lulu's translating," Olly explained. "She's not happy with you." He bent further down with a slight grimace to dislodge the rocks, pinning me to the mountainside — he was still hurt.

Based on his face and the sheer volume of chittering coming from Ciacha, I felt that may be an understatement on Olly's part — that maybe more curses were involved. A lot of them. I didn't speak spider, and Osiet wasn't volunteering anything but orbital bombardment, so I had to go with it.

"I'm not particularly fond of *her*, either." I glared as he freed my other wrist. She'd been none too gentle when she'd swatted Olly into the rocks. And when she tried to stab me. And...

"Those were her babies," Olly interrupted my scowling, his voice flat. "She was defending her brood."

Well. Shit.

I noticed them when I sat up — little skitterers clinging to her swollen abdomen. The ones who hadn't gone pop-kablewy from Bridge's blaze of glory. Clearing more debris from my feet, I tried to ignore them and instead noticed something else entirely that I didn't like — shackling webs strung around Olly's feet and tied to his wrists.

I scrabbled back and leapt to my feet, bolts charging with a hum as I readied to strike.

Fast as I was, Ciacha was faster.

She'd closed the distance in a silent flash. The sharpened point of one foreleg was at my throat in an instant while another primed to skewer Olly.

I froze, weighing my options. Become a prisoner, or save myself and lose Olly. Neither were good choices.

Osiet Ros offered a third, showing me an infinitesimal speck in orbit — no bigger than a grain of rice, but made of pure metal and capable of surviving atmospheric entry. "It will never see it coming." Thunder laughed as gleeful words appeared, tugging at the orbital bullet.

Ciacha chittered as I thought, pressing the point ever so slightly as Olly translated: "In freeing you, I bargain for the freedom of my own. Swear it so," Olly paused, his eyes meeting mine, "or I shall bury you again."

"Take the shot while you may," the words of Osiet Ros glowed.

Is it being controlled? I silently asked my rider.

Motes swirled in delayed deliberation, finally revealing an answer: "No."

She could have killed both of us at any time and didn't. I relaxed my guard, charge draining from the knuckle busters. Slowly, I raised my hands.

"Fool," my rider rumbled an echo, retreating deeper into my heart now that the battle Ros so loved abated. The presence vanished, but I still felt the orbital munitions in my brain — waiting, poised to strike.

As Ciacha lashed my arms and legs together proficiently with her web, I glanced toward the rings arching overhead as night on this planetoid darkened the sky — bits of waiting death glistened in the waning light.

Olly and I were now her prisoners. As we marched who knows where, I couldn't help but wonder: *where's Luna?*

/06/

"Can she understand us?" We'd been walking well into the cycle of dark, following along the steel web tethering us to our captor. Stumbling really. Really missed the night vision stored in my pack — confiscated with my busters.

"Not rightly sure," Olly said, considering. He tilted his head like he was listening — probably to his rider. I guess they were on better terms again after the almost dying bit. "I just go non-threatening when she seems in a stabby mood."

"Seems to work," I said, keeping an eye on our surroundings as best I could in the dark. If we were able to make a break for it, I wanted to know which way to go. We'd gone about five klicks down the scrabble and around a cliff — to the left and away from the nest I'd bombarded. "You see Javier anywhere?"

"He tossed a scratched tile on me before the slide," Olly replied. Probably what saved his life. "Went for you next. I'm not sure after that." Olly frowned, obviously worried. "Ciacha pulled me out after. Said she felt me under the rocks," he explained. "Vibrations, I think. You too."

"But not Luna…" I trailed off, thinking. Either he was dead or deeper in the rubble than a spider could feel. Or he'd gotten out ahead of Olly and made himself scarce. "He'd be good at that," I thought out loud. In another life, I'd heard he'd been Spec4 Mafia.

"Good at what?" Olly had been twisting and tugging at his binds as we marched, unable to get them undone — too much play to snap, not enough to do much other than walk. Smart.

"Making himself scarce," I said, inspecting our shackles. Tensile steel — essentially — fixed to us with a gummy goo that gave but never broke. I didn't even try to slip them — no point. If Olly's strength couldn't break through them, mine was no match.

"Luna wouldn't leave us," Olly insisted. "He's a good man, good brother." I didn't think he'd left us for dead, not by a long shot. But shit never goes the way you plan after the first bullet — or meteor — is fired.

"He wouldn't," I agreed, but — in case Ciacha *could* understand us — I held my tongue, changing the subject. "Kinda hypocritical, don't you think?" I held up my bound hands. "Her bargaining for freedom while taking us hostage?"

"Does kinda seem not right," Olly nodded. "I might have missed something in the translation, though." He shrugged, his silhouette in the night odd without his nuke and the doom tube.

I eyed our weapons strapped to the backside of our captor as we trailed behind. The remnants of her brood rode upon her back as well, their many eyes fixed upon us as we stumbled forward nearly blind. Hate radiated from their incessant gaze as hundreds of red dots glowed eerily in the dark, burning into me.

The cable pulled taut, vibrating through to our binds and into our bones: *ALARM*.

Head on swivel, I'd be damned if I could see anything — blind without my goggles. I heard it, though, rocks clattering from above in the night and then the tell-tale hiss of the necrobots. Shadows rose all along the ridge line, outlined only in starlight.

We were surrounded.

And the world exploded in front of us, reanimate husks bursting from the ground in a flurry of limbs and violence. Our guide leapt left — jerking us off our feet — while flinging our weapon sack right to distract the attacker. Her young scurried down our lead line and over us, their furry legs causing me to cringe as they made their escape.

Her young safely away from immediate violence, Ciacha cut the tether. Our shackling strands came free — still bound around our hands and feet, but no longer tied together. Olly and I scattered, gaining our bearing.

Ciacha was engaging the enemy — reared on hind legs wrestling a monstrously large necrobot as two more webbed down from the cliff top.

"I'll get the weapons," I called to Olly. "You get to bashing," I threw my hands toward Ciacha.

"Ro'er," Olly called, leaping toward the fray. Unencumbered, he was damn fast — even shackled— already halfway there as I dashed for our kit. Barehanded, the big man was still devastating, while I...well, wasn't. I needed the busters or *something* against anything this large.

"You do not." Golden motes formed the words of thunder. I wasn't sure if Osiet was *always* watching, but silently, or if adrenaline spikes attracted my rider. Were all the Eshali like this?

Ros didn't answer, simply showed me rocks tumbling in space that could easily be brought to serve, should I but allow it. Tempting me. Taunting me.

"You've no need of meager weapons." Another subtitled rumble nearly lost in the shockwave of another necrobot landing between me and salvation. "Why limit yourself? My last did not." Images flashed — one in particular standing out.

The thoughts floating in my brain distracted me for a split second too long as the enemy swiped to the side, sending me sprawling through the dirt and rocks.

Olly fared much better, his shackles making the perfect take-down tool. He pulled the steel web taut between his fists, parrying the stabbing strike of the necrobot and spinning to the outside as it passed. The second was quick to strike at Olly's back, but he turned to catch that one with the web and wrap it around the outstretched leg, pulling the over-extended spider off-base — putting his shoulder into it for a throw.

I don't think there are many people capable of pulling off Kali shit on a spider the size of a car, but Olly Bostock is one of them. Olly spun, sending the flailing fury flying at the larger necrobot grappling with Ciacha.

Show off. It gave her the break she needed, though, forcing the enemy spider off balance and onto its back. She mounted for the kill.

My own would-be killer advanced as I crouched defensively on the rocky terrain. I took a cue from Olly and stretched my bindings taut — ready to catch its strike — but instead of waiting for it, I took initiative. I didn't have Olly's strength, but I did have speed. Dust kicked as I dashed in under the necrobot's first lunging strike, parrying it upward to slide it over my head. I ducked under the second leg as it ran and grabbed it from behind to pull myself up.

Planting a foot, I sprang up top to straddle the spider's back — taking it for a ride. Somehow, in that intervening span, I noticed Olly had managed to rip not one but two forelegs off the smallest necrobot he faced, and began using them as poi — deflecting strikes and returning them even easier.

The spider I rode bucked, trying to throw me. I looped my bindings over its head and around its neck as it rolled against boulders, trying to scrape me off. Another loop around its neck as my back got torn up by the rock face, I held firm, pulling my choke even tighter.

Thing is, chokes don't exactly work on the necrobots, seeing as they don't exactly breathe. However, their heads *do* pop clean off if you pull tight enough — and I summoned every ounce of strength and leverage I could muster to do just that.

Pop.

With a little crunch and a lot of satisfaction. Sadistic glee from my rider tickled my brain as the husk spasmed and jerked, flinging me free before collapsing into stillness.

More necrobots descended on Olly and Ciacha, with further reinforcements crawling down the cliff. Olly speared one with a stolen leg as it leapt, sending it limp. The other leg he brandished to keep a long-limbed, black carapaced necrobot at bay while Ciacha stabbed at it from above with her own spearing leg. Two small ones took to her back and began to bite — she leapt and spun to try to fling them free. The pair wouldn't last, effective as they were — not in a battle of attrition like this. There were just too many.

"Then even the odds," the glowing words whispered violence. I could feel Osiet Ros growing more and more present as the battle pitched. More eager for me to strike out with my gift.

But I would not. I *would*, however, even the odds. My way.

Pain shot up my arm as I pushed off the ground, quickly muted as I sprinted for our weapons.

That can't be good. The thought briefly flirted, vying for my attention, but I'd have to revisit it later. More pressing was the matter of surviving.

"I hope the hopper's full," I muttered as I tore frantically at the web sack spun around our gear, the hot blood covering my hands wet the strands, turning them to mush as I dug. I slammed the switch buried in webbing and heard the twelve-phase hum to life as I ripped the barrel free.

"Get low!" I shouted at Olly and Ciacha — if she could understand me — as I trained the doom tube their direction. Two counts later, I unleashed hell, hoping Olly had heard and gone flat on the ground. I couldn't lug the nuke pack around, but I could damn well use the twelve-phase as a stationary gun placement.

The night lit up bright with tracers from the rail gun burning through the air, illuminating the carnage. I felt Osiet Ros smile with my face and rip a maniacal laugh from my throat as I squeezed the trigger. Bits and pieces of necrobot flew as I launched steely death over my best friend's head, their goo painting the rocks purple.

As much as I braced myself, though, I couldn't hold aim — the doom tube kicks like a mother... I felt my arm squish and spurt as my grip only grew tighter, enhanced by my rider, trying to target the necrobots skittering up the rocks. How Olly managed this while running, I was at a loss. The hopper ran dry, tail unable to reload.

The whuffing hum gave way to silence as the doom tube begged to be fed. One spider rose in the silence, a shadow racing toward me lightning quick.

"Kel, look out!" Olly called out from the midst of ruination, trying to run after the shadow heading my way — brought short by a limp.

Instinctively, I aimed and pulled the trigger, but to no avail — only empty sputter as the hopper whined. I braced for the shadow's strike as one pointed limb shot forward toward me, glinting striped orange in the starlight.

CRUNCH followed by steaming goop splattering my neck as I came face to face with Ciacha, her thrust skewering a necrobot I'd not seen. Her red eyes looking into mine, I felt a moment of understanding as the air around her vibrated.

"Thank you," I hazarded a reply, unmoving. Slowly, her foreleg withdrew from the slain necrobot, allowing it to collapse behind me.

Neither of us moved until she looked down at the doom tube in my hands. I tried to drop it, but my hand refused to obey — my grip locked in place, pulling an empty trigger.

"Stop it," I said aloud, trying to regain control. "Let go." Osiet had snuck through in the fight, taking parts of me under control.

"You do not wish me to let go," the thunder purred. "I assure you."

"Kel," Olly approached cautiously. Ciacha seemed to grow more agitated.

"Let go," I said again. "Olly, take it, bro. I can't open my hand."

"I got you." Olly slipped under Ciacha's legs as non-threateningly as possible. Hands open, moving slowly. She twitched, but did not strike. Slowly, he pulled my hand off the trigger with a squish and a scream.

The scream came from me. The moment Olly touched me, Osiet Ros let go of whatever the hell it was the rider had done. Wave after wave of pain tore through me.

"As I said," the words inverted in the searing pain. A roar of blood ripped at my ears, drowning the world for a moment.

"Kel," Olly's voice held concern. "Kellan!" He'd caught me as I dropped, unable to stand after Osiet Ros withdrew whatever had kept me upright.

"I'm here," I managed through the pain. "Grab my IFAK." I nodded to the webbing sack I'd ripped open. Could use painkillers, and something to stop the bleeding I seemed to be doing would be great. "Get the NODs, too," I added. "If she'll let you," I spared a glance at the hovering spider. I'd like to see if we were attacked again.

"You brought night vision?" Olly hadn't been regiment before getting railroaded. Shit like this was why you always took your goggles — never knew when you'd be stuck out in the dark.

Worse — stuck out in the dark with undead spiders erupting from the pitch black ground you're walking on. Talk about home field advantage. At least our...captor? Guide? Ally? I wasn't sure what Ciacha was exactly...could sense them in the endless night. How, I wasn't sure.

Pain lanced through me again. I squeezed my eyes shut as the stars came alight behind my eyes. I heard Olly start rummaging. Surprisingly, Ciacha did let him near the gear. Maybe she did understand us. I'd have to keep that in mind. She swayed rhythmically as she stood over us, occasionally looking down at me, but for the most part she seemed to be keeping watch.

"Pill pack all you got?" Olly ripped open the packet he'd fished out and dumped it in my mouth. Some cheap painkillers and a couple other things that might keep me alive later. For now, though, I was focused on the pain — I choked them down while he kept looking for the goggles.

"Canteen cup," I added when Olly'd come up empty.

"Why are..." He pulled out the pouch with the tin cup that held my night optics.

"Keeps 'em from getting broke." I coughed, tasting the tang of blood again. "You know. Hard landings, bullets," I went on, "and..."

"Not rockslides," Olly interrupted before I could say just that, holding out the crumpled cup.

Well damn. It wasn't supposed to rattle like that.

/07/

To say I was banged up was an understatement. After Olly'd run out of combat bandages for my, let's just say, pulped arms and administered all the first aid he was able to, Ciacha stepped in.

The giant spider surprisingly made a good nurse — deftly packing open wounds with soft, gauzy webs then wrapping them with stouter strands. In the process, I learned she actually had hooklike fingers on her second legs for fine thread manipulation.

For my apparently busted legs, Olly broke off bits of the dead for Ciacha to splint to me. How the hell had I been functioning that long?

Thunder laughed, and I knew Osiet had done something to push beyond my limits. Infinitely amused by my suffering, I'd begun to think all Osiet Ros knew how to do was laugh in peals of thunder.

The storm quieted a moment and the dead language began, rattled off by the husky whisper of my rider. No translation provided, but by the tone, none was required. I likely didn't want to know what exactly was said; the tone was enough. It reminded me of an ex, in fact — Liat always cursed me out in Hebrew.

Some things are universal.

Like the treatment of an invalid.

I'd protested. I could walk, damnit. But found myself unwillingly hoisted to the back of a giant spider — her brood now keeping me company.

Most still hated me — I could *feel* it in their persistent gaze — but a couple were somewhat neutral. One particularly brave one crawled right up to me and just stared. Mandibles worked as the spider swayed — was it trying to talk?

"And who are you?" I reached out a bandaged hand to the little fellow as I would a dog — it was roughly the size of one.

"I'd say that's Fred," Olly called up.

"Lulu translate that for you?" The spiders had an odd way of communicating. I'd begun to suspect it was more than the chittery clicks.

"No," Olly said. "But it's a good name. Had a horse named Fred," he nodded. "Three of them, actually," he cocked his head in thought.

"That's just lazy," I called down to the big man as he ambled alongside our guard. After the fight, she'd dispensed with the tow-line — a modicum of respect and understanding earned? Or was I tether enough? — but the shackles remained.

"Is not!" He panted a little bit. It had been hours since the fight, and I could see faint lightning in the sky that heralded the dawn. "Fred's a perfectly good name. Was good enough for my rocking horse, it's good enough for him."

"Your rocking..." I started, but shut my trap. Didn't feel like getting in any deeper. "Well, how about it?" The little spider crept up to my outstretched hand and probed it with its foreleg. "Fred," I said again now that it touched me.

The little spider felt the name and shook its abdomen side to side before jumping — the chittering sound it made seemed agreeable, at least.

"I think he likes it, Kel," Olly laughed.

"How do you know it's a he?" There were no obvious markers in coloration — browns and blacks with orangey stripes like his mama — Fred could be a she for all we knew. The only distinctive mark of any kind was the splotch of blue above his larger left eye in the shape of a raised brow, giving him a perpetually quizzical expression.

"His name's Fred," Olly replied. "That's how," he nodded, certain in his assertion.

"Of course," I said. *'Cause that's exactly how that works*, I kept to myself as Fred decided to take a closer look, climbing into my lap. I froze, not wanting to trigger any sort of response from the little spider, the little spider's siblings, or their mother, for that matter.

The dog-sized Fred poked at me with hairy legs, prodding the bandages and ministrations of his mother before crawling up and over to my back — making a lap before settling in mine. Vibrating all the while.

Cozy. The word came unbidden to mind as had the earlier alarm from Ciacha.

"I think we're coming up on something," Olly hollered up. I couldn't see a damn thing except the dust we kicked, facing backward on the spider. "Looks like another nest."

Fantastic.

Visions of rocks tumbled in my head — lazily spinning above this cursed planet. Waiting for *some* reason to fall.

I said no, I preempted the tempting rumble of Osiet Ros. I'd not cause any more cataclysms if I could help it.

As we walked, I saw the signs of the spiders — goo gobbed on a rock here and there, tripwires and trap lines skirted by our guide, and brief glimpses of outlines atop the ridges. The kind too quick to actually see — only noticed by the sudden lack of movement as the brain caught up. One of them looked smaller than the rest, though, and I wondered.

"It's huge!" Olly'd apparently caught sight of more than scant signs. "You won't believe it," he added as he hitched a ride on Ciacha's back, coming to sit beside me.

I craned my neck around, trying to see why as the ground vanished behind us, leaving only open air. Guess that answered my question. Ciacha had walked us out over the edge on webs of the thinnest thread — barely visible in the early light. Every now and then, I caught a glimmer of the gossamer vibrating as we crossed into the canyon. I decided it was better for the moment not to look — too many rickety ladders shimmied across rooftops.

"Hi Fred," Olly said as he scratched the little guy's head. In response, Fred vibrated, leaking a little webbing from his spinnerets all over my lap.

"Ewwww, Fred!" I tried to wipe the web goo off, but, of course, it stuck. That's what it was for.

"Oh, don't be like that, Kel," Olly cooed. "He can't help it if he gets excited for scratches." Olly continued with the petting, getting Fred all worked up to the point he jumped on the big man.

"How is it," I began, "you've been splatting spiders every day since training and *him* you treat like a puppy?"

"Easy," he smiled. "Fred ain't tried to kill me." Olly scratched under his chin. "Have you, boy? Have you?" Excited spider noises followed all the attention.

One of a kind, our Olly. He kept fawning all over Fred as the other younglings looked on, tentatively creeping forward to see what the commotion was about. Olly crouched to share the pets...

Halt tingled up my spine, and our ride did — hanging on a thread in the open air. Chittering rose in an echo.

"Checkpoint challenge," Olly whispered — voicing what info Lulu had provided.

"I kinda got that vibe," I whispered back. "Lulu saying anything else?"

Olly shook his head once, scanning for the guards.

Ciacha moved slightly to respond, taking her second leg — the one with the deft fingers she'd used to wrap my wounds — strumming the strand on which she stood, causing it to sing.

Around us, the canyon walls sang with response — harmonics mixed with staccatoed chitters. A veritable symphony of spiders whose music seeped into my bones.

"Hang on tight," Olly said, grabbing onto my lashings himself as the world tilted under us.

Ciacha flipped under the webbing she'd been walking on, tying off with new using her hind legs — beginning our descent. The only thing I can compare it to is fast-roping out of a Chinook, except I could do fuck-all about it — just along for the ride. And this one was a hell of a lot longer than ninety feet. I had time to admire the scenery as we plummeted to the ground below.

Reminded me a bit of the cliff dwellings in Mesa Verde — if each hole in the rock were filled with funnel webs. The entire face was covered in the gauzy white stuff. And in each, a dark body perched — come to see who'd come calling — with more hiding deeper inside. Spiders of every size worked their way around the interconnected strands with uncanny speed and agility — the network hummed with song as they did. The entire colony would know of our arrival.

I was only able to grasp the full scope of the spider settlement when Ciacha spun 'round during descent. Dizzying as that was, it provided a panoramic view of the encampment webs devouring the canyon walls. The mountain nest of the necrobots and their captives wasn't a tenth this size.

"What kind of hell world did they spit us out on?" I couldn't help the utterance, but damn. If these all became necrobots, or worse — decided we were their enemy as a whole...

"Lulu doesn't have a name for it," Olly piped up. "Says it's unlike their kind to mass. Could get messy, though," he agreed with my unspoken thought.

"Strike the heart!" The peal of thunder forced its way to the front of my brain, flashing words before my face before I could suppress it.

Olly laid a hand on my arm, shaking his head when my eyes met his — face etched with concern. He'd seen the look likely plastered on my face too many times. I'd have to be careful to keep Osiet's bloodlust in check.

As we descended, the route sealed behind us, layer after layer of webbing restrung across. Some strands were obvious, others nearly invisible. Interspersed throughout, I saw clumps of fat white sacks looking precariously placed. I wondered what sort of surprises they contained.

"They're defending from the air," I thought aloud, craning my neck to see. Along walls, just below the canyon rim, I saw the sentries — at least their shadows. These spiders blended in well with the rocks — rusty reds and browns, broken by mottled black and tans. Quiet and small. Likely agile on the defensive trapeze the spiders had constructed.

"The Avispa." The name flashed before my eyes again. Osiet Ros' terseness explaining little.

"Ros just rumbled 'Avispa,'" I turned to Olly. "Mean anything to Lulu?"

"Ick," Olly grimaced. "He just replayed this NatGeo episode I saw when I was a kid. Big ass wasps stabbing tarantulas," he gacked, "laying eggs in 'em."

"Parasites," Ros kindly provided. "Devour the hosts from within and conscript their remains." My rider showed images of necrobot spiders bursting into swarms of flying death. That sure as hell wasn't in my briefing.

"That's why they're massing," Olly went on. "Alone, they don't stand a goddamn chance." He looked around at the caves in the cliffside, the webbing strung all around. Made sense – overcome a tactically superior enemy with sheer numbers. These spiders seemed clever as well – learning to adapt and survive.

The world went right again as Ciacha touched down on the canyon floor. Olly started to hop off, but she barred his way, chittering a warning.

"If you say so," he said, sitting back down. He made to scratch one of the spiderlings — not Fred, I thought. Some of the others had come around to the big man's affections, but they skittered to the ground covered in soft, batteny webs. A few of the clumps wiggled, causing the young ones to glee and pounce, sinking their mandibles into the sack lunches – live prey to draw out their predatory instincts.

My stomach turned as they made hideous slurping sounds between high-pitched, joyous noises. I swallowed back bile as the lumps quickly dissolved — the brood had been hungry.

I didn't want to know what they'd just eaten, though Ros kept flashing the earlier images of entrails being gorged upon every damn time I blinked. *Stop it!*

More spiders approached from behind — red-carapaced and exceptionally long-limbed — reaching toward us with strands strung between their probing legs. Their mandibles glistened as they clacked together, spreading venomous wetness.

Oh shit.

/08/

Ciacha leapt and spun, albeit staggering a little drunken on the landing — knocking the wrappings away.

I guess we weren't dessert after all. Or she was hogging us to herself.

Ferocious chittering and gesturing of legs cowed the red spiders, sullenly backing away, their abdomens clutched in a manner that bespoke hunger.

"This food bites," Olly translated. "They are war-makers I wish to recruit."

Food. Great.

"Did I not apprise you of their culinary predilections?" Words of admonition scrawled in my brain as I felt Ciacha set off who knows where, echoed by reminders of the warnings offered before.

"You did mention that," I said through gritted teeth, carefully looking around to see if Olly was listening. "And if they do, stick that tungsten through my brain," I added when I saw him busy looking for more would-be diners approaching Ciacha's six. I didn't like the notion of biting the bullet, but like my rider had said — I'd never see this one coming.

"And the rest?" Osiet Ros widened the orbital view floating in the back of my brain, cherry-picking which bits of debris to descend. The Eshali delighted at the prospect of a repeat apocalypse.

I declined to answer. My earlier bombardment had cost enough of my soul — more than I'd thought. The radioed cries of my dying brothers — shitbags though they were — still haunted me. I was a soldier, but I did not share my rider's zeal for death-dealing.

I just did what needed done.

"As do we all," the cryptic words formed in swirls over the dead tongue, licking my brain before fading — my rider's presence retreating once more. Probably out scouting rocks to drop on my head — however that worked. Distantly, the telltale thunder rumbled.

We lurched as Ciacha missed a step, her leg twitching a second before falling back in line. Not surprising, considering she'd force marched all night — not sure how many klicks we'd come — after two fights and a landslide and who knew what before that. A mother's determination isn't to be underestimated.

I looked out over the camp — that's what this was. It wasn't a nest or a home. These were makeshift dwellings spread through the entirety of the canyon — spider stacked on top of spider, hungry and desperate. I saw two scrabble off to the side — a fat-bodied brown spider with hairy legs tackled a lanky yellow and black as it tried to suck on one of the lumpy sack lunches. There wasn't enough to go around — whatever it was they ate.

Come to think of it, I hadn't seen anything alive on this damned hunk of rock except us and now these spiders. The necrobots didn't count — animate isn't necessarily alive.

"What'd ya think's in the lumps?" Olly asked real quietlike. He'd seen the fight, too.

"Don't wanna know," I said. I told myself they looked too small to be men. Repeatedly.

The ground was littered with the bundles — and there hadn't been that many of us come through — but still, there were even more hungry spiders sucking at them. Hunger had been gnawing at the back of my mind, but nah, I was good.

Hairy legs wasn't, though. The lanky yellow spider'd turned the tide on him — was it a him? Let's just say it was a him — slick carapace foreleg slicing through the bulky brown's thorax, cutting two legs off one side. Blueish-purple blood sprayed from the wound, sending the emaciated onlookers into a frenzy, devouring the stricken spider as its hairy legs curled in on themselves in death.

"Real friendly," Olly opined.

"Could've been us," I said, voice hollow. "Had Ciacha not intervened."

"She likes us," Olly deluded himself.

"She has plans for us," I reminded him. "There's a difference." We were useful weapons.

They were all the same — the major, Command, our arachnid patron here. Hell, even our Eshali riders — each found us useful, and so they kept us around — until we broke.

"I will not discard you," golden motes floated again. They felt...soothing? "On this, you have my oath." Was Osiet trying to comfort me?

"I have only acted in your best interests," my rider stiffened, subtitles shattering like brittle sand taken by the wind. "Since the very start."

"Funny way of showing it," I grumbled, testing my mangled limbs — used far beyond flesh's limits.

"Thou didst not perish, thanks to my bolstering."

Before I could mouth off, Ciacha stopped.

We were there.

There was like anywhere else in this forsaken camp, except here the webs seemed to spiral and swerve — stretching out in every direction. Also, the spiders here seemed more...dignified, I suppose, is the best way to put it.

None of them wore top hats, monocles, or anything so absurd, but they carried themselves with a refined grace — no two alike — deliberate in their movements.

"Elders, Lulu says," Olly whispered barely over the rising music.

"I think the blood loss is getting to me," half to myself. I legit heard music. Orchestral type. It began to swell as an elder with a bleached-white carapace gestured with a foreleg as a hind leg quivered — overtaking the chittering I heard bantering back and forth. Ciacha lowered herself before the gathered spiders.

"Time to get off," Olly translated as he loosened my improvised straps, helping me slide down.

I stood there, still bleeding — seeping really — through the dressings on my mangled limbs as the pulped flesh took pressure again — staining the webs holding me together red in growing splotches.

The pervasive music had grown louder when my feet touched the ground, coming in contact with the white webbing. Olly seemed to notice it as well, cocking his head to listen as he helped hold me up. It usually meant Lulu was talking to him, but maybe this time it was the spiders' song.

Sweeping notes swelled as the white spider gestured with its front legs, raising higher than the surrounding spiders — already larger than most, this only served to make it more imposing. On it went in animated fashion, until a moment of crescendo stunned the others to silence.

I couldn't understand what had been said — I thought they had been arguing, the music felt quite tense — or really by whom, and I wasn't about to break the silence by asking Olly if he caught all that. Thankfully, it was broken for me as a sad song began to sway hold in the hush.

There was this hot chick in college I was trying to ask out, while back. Turned out she was a theater major, so I decided to see one of the plays she was in — some musical. Don't ask me what the name was — there were trees and a witch and a wolf. I didn't really get it, but now I sorta did as I listened to the spiders' song in my bones.

I felt the despair of the mother making the music. She wept for her dead children. She wept for her live children now with no home and no hope. She raged at the enemy that had stolen her mate — used his corpse as a weapon alongside her brothers' and mother's. Her father had fought the invaders with their sting and buzz, failing to overcome the onslaught — not enough of him left to reanimate. The Avispa — flying terrors, unholy nightmares that had enslaved her clan — forced them to die and fight and die again with no song

.

Tears welled in my eyes, moved as I was by her plight. Chords struck out at my heart, rousing emotions I'd long ignored. The song went on.

Sadness and fear gave way to hatred as she'd made her escape in the night — leaving everything behind. Pain, too, throbbed in chorus. She'd been hurt. Something sharp, maybe. It was hard to tell specifics as I was carried along by the flood of emotion.

Taken as I was, I hadn't realized the song now sung belonged to Ciacha. Hadn't realized just how much she'd been through before she'd dug us out. We were getting to that part now as I felt the rocks fall again, wiping out the nest we'd found. Pure rage swelled, cresting the tide of sadness that had washed over us. A stilted staccato, nearly militaristic march, took over the song as Ciacha plucked the strands of web violently now — our part.

I felt the eyes of all the spiders gathered turn to us — all dozen times eight of 'em — pinning us in place. Hatred laced with judgment. But from a few, a thread of hope as they subtly stroked the web in response to the musical tale as she laid out her planned alliance.

'*This food bites,*' I remembered Olly's translated words.

My feet itched to move — to flee — but still I stood, not letting them see me flinch. Never show fear — it'll be the death of you. It'd been drilled in me since regiment — don't let them catch you. Escape. Evade. Don't get caught.

Don't get caught. I'd ingloriously failed at that part. Now I stood face to face with — no, not the enemy. Not the true enemy. I had to rethink that. The necrobots that had tried to kill me on this rock and so many others weren't attacking me by choice. They were dead, stripped of all will and malice.

The sapphire spider, though... he was full of malice. Malice and hatred oozed from him as he cut Ciacha's song off with a discordant riff.

"*Them!?*" his song raged, skittering close enough to breathe. "*These weak-fleshes killed Songless?*" Disbelief and doubt evident in the harmonies.

Is that what they called the necrobots? I wondered as I stood stock still, trying to hold in my own blood, no emotion on my face. Never show fear. Instead, I studied the intricacies of the jewel-toned carapace invading my personal space. Admittedly it was a pretty color with subtle patterning of black lines, gradually thickening to all black at the joints. Small hairs bristled as it exhaled in my face, mandibles clicking just out of chewing distance.

I'd been up close and personal with far too many spiders for my liking, but at least this one wasn't trying to kill me — yet. It examined me as I examined it, rows of black eyes boring into me.

"*His kind fling metal death near and far,*" the song sang. "*And from above. I wish us to make use of these war-makers in ou...*"

Sapphire quivered at the mention of the meteors. Then struck.

I toppled back fast, thrown clear by Olly as shining blue jaws snapped shut where my head once was. Fast as it had happened, it felt like I swam in molasses. Sluggish barely begins to describe how delayed my reaction was. Olly was on top of it, though — literally — holding the blue's mandibles closed with his meaty hands.

In from the sides, two spiders rushed — guards, I presumed. Fugly ones at that. Long brown faces frozen in scowls and crowned with horns. Perfect for blending into rocks and trees. They forced themselves between the furious sapphire and my knocked-flat-ass while Olly rolled clear of the cluster — spreading a trapping web over the attacker.

"*Saizsir,*" a sharp chord cut, "*compose yourself!*"

"I demand they pay for the deaths of my clutch!" Saizsir — apparently that was the angry spider's name — thrashed, the web net drawing tight around its legs.

"Their penance is yet ungiven," I felt from the bleached elder.

"Have them stack the bodies of Songless in measure to your loss, Saizsir," Ciacha offered. *"As I plan to."*

The spider called Saizsir struggled, flinging through the web net a sack, which landed squarely at my feet. Seeing inside, I felt ill.

"See what they have done!" The sapphire spider stilled in sadness. *"I barely survived their wanton destruction from above. My young never..."* the spider quivered, trailing off. *"Penance? No penance can atone for this."* Eight sorrowful eyes bored into me.

Cautiously, one of the interceding guards upended the sack, spilling the contents. A leg, broken off at the joint. A bit of mandible stuck out oddly from half a head. A crushed abdomen, never allowed to grow fat. Part after broken body part emptied from the sack — hundreds of them — all gleaming the same gemstone blue.

Thunder roared in my head, warring with my own maelstrom of emotion.

Too much, too close. All went slack. I fell.

"Kel," Olly muffled through cotton balls. "Kellan..." he faded into the storm.

It'd broken sudden on the busted ass mountain the Chinook dumped us out on. Back in Regiment, some slope we probably shouldn't have been taking a walk on. But...that's how it went.

Shit went sideways; we cleaned it up. Made sure no one made off with our boys — and blew the hell out of whatever gear hadn't already been toast.

Not that we could see a damn thing, but hey — they couldn't either. Most importantly, couldn't see us. Idiots kept firing where they thought we were — nice of them to give their location like that. We'd pop them every now and then. Keep 'em guessing.

"Sow the chaotic seeds and thin the ranks," approving words shimmered. I guess Osiet Ros liked the home movie running through my skull as much as the real deal.

"Popcorn?" I offered. "Any reason you picked this one in particular?" Not that any were particularly *good*, just this one never sat right.

"I chose it not." My rider left it hanging, declining my offer of mental popcorn.

So I did, huh? Maybe I could shift gears to a titty club off-base. Maybe one with an all-you-can-eat buffet. I'd tried to ignore it, but I was starving.

"Repast with the spiderlings you grow fond of." Blue ice sparkled. Again with the force-fed images of entrails being slurped and faces in the sack lunches Ciacha's kids ate up.

Meanwhile, the mountainside stormed on, unrelenting. My ass had fallen in water at some point, squelching along. Frozen. So cold and wet I just couldn't get warm. I wasn't sure my feet were actually working, but I was moving so I guess they were.

Days. Hours unending.

Movement to contact. Neutralize the threat. Pop-pop. Move on. Next. Pop-pop.

We'd been fishing in the fog...no, that was another mission. Another guy. All my guys.

G told me about fishing in the fog once. Wait. His ass wasn't on that mountain with me — never in my unit — but might as well have been.

Same shit, different deployment. Cold and wet, then hot and dry. Cold. Hot. All of us went wherever we got pointed.

Cold. So cold. Why weren't my fingers working? Squeeze the trigger. BANG. Okay, at least one's working.

Hot. So hot. My throat burned in the air.

Distant thunder rumbled in my heart. A good rain would have been nice about then. So hot. The rain never came.

Burning sand in my eyes. Everything on fire.

Everything on fire.

Fire from the sky.

A dead tongue licked my ear.

"Yes."

/09/

"NO!" I screamed, bolting upright in darkness.

"What did you...I do?" Silence. At least the world hadn't ended, I thought. Hard to tell when you can't see your hand in front of your face.

Not that *that* was easy right then. Still hurt like hell, but I felt my hand move, then touched my face with it. Bad idea.

"Ah fuck." My pulped nose went squish, making a gritty noise in my head, sounding like — I shit you not — styrofoam snapping and grinding. That was a new one. Teeth loose, also new.

Blood tasted the same, though. Some things don't change.

Horrific new sounds aside, I caught snatches of the pervasive music I'd heard since arriving at the spider camp mixed with familiar chittering. Were they coming?

"Olly," I tried quietly, hoping the big fella was close. If he was here he'd've said he was when I screamed — if he could. Maybe he was hard asleep.

Nothing. Wishful thinking, I knew.

I tested my hands in the darkness, ignoring the stabs of pain now encroaching on my consciousness. Still bound, naturally, but somewhat cooperative. Legs — also bound — much less so on the cooperation.

The chittering grew closer, echoing strangely down what I assumed to be a hall — tunnel maybe. No light to speak of, even after my eyes had time to adjust. No sun, no stars, no faint shimmer of death waiting above. Where had they stashed me? The walls felt...damp? Not quite sticky, but it did feel like they were covered in some kind of web.

Yay, spider spit. I didn't have time to feel my way around the room, getting my bearings — even if my legs did work. I'd have to wait for something to poke its head out and go boo.

"If you wish to see," the words floated before me, "all you need do is ask."

"At what cost?" The Eshali always extracted a price.

Hadn't I paid enough?

"Your death benefits me not," the words flowed into green sparkles lining the edges of the room in a weird sort of wireframe contour mish-map.

"Shoulda told me you could do that," I muttered in darkness, scoping the room out as I lay in wait. Wasn't much to see at any rate. Small box like any cell, but...round. Ish. One wall was kinda straight, but the opposite curved away from me. The straight one was the sticky, spider-snot-covered one — kinda squishy like my nose. No door to be seen, but at least I could see in the darkness. Would've been handy on the march. What other tricks was my rider hiding?

"You sought only speed, strength, and the resiliency to match," Osiet's words glowed in the overlay. "You asked not to see."

"What are you, a lawyer?" I knew the Eshali were sticklers, but that was just petty. Sure, hadn't come up before — always had my NODs — but still could have said.

"I am of order and rule," scrolled below the wall I watched — gut said that was still the way out — the word *rule* oddly emphasized.

"Didn't ask to be a walking apocalypse either," I shot. "Gave me plenty of that."

"How little you understand me," the thunder in my heart prickled, the dancing motes forming the words took on a sharp edge as well. "Balance is my nature." The unhinged battle maniac was serious.

"Fucked up balance." Meteors exploded in my mind.

"At the extremes, yes," Ros begrudgingly acknowledged — countering the scarring devastation seared in my brain with images of fertile valleys and overflowing abundance. Fruit ripening sweetly on heavily laden vines and trees — so plentiful the boughs and branches threatened to snap.

"Always extreme with you," I muttered. Screams of the dying I'd condemned drowning my voice.

"The penchant for violence lies not with me." Doubling down on the verdant imagery, kicking it up a notch with a pleasant wind whistling through the dappled leaves I could spend a lifetime under.

Reverie cut short as the sounds of branches scraping against one another changed to chittering. "They come, ready yourself."

I felt the urge to kill rise within me, stoked by my rider. Source or not, Ros certainly enjoyed the violence.

The wall bulged inward as the rustling branches vanished, replaced by the horns of the fugly guard in the limning green light of the Eshali's night vision.

"Now," the word flashed, circling the target.

I struck.

All pain and fatigue vanished as my rider force-fed adrenaline straight to my systems. Elsewhere in ignored parts of my anatomy, warning bells and alarms sounded tenfold, but, given the situation, were ignored. There'd be time for pain later so long as there *was* a later.

Survive. Escape. Evade.

Those were the priorities in this situation. I wasn't going out like...

"Whoa, Kel!" Olly interceded between me and fug-face, jumping under and through the spider's legs. "Easy does."

Big, meaty arms wrapped around me mid-strike, firmly refusing to let the punch through as my body caught up to my consciousness.

"Olly?" He wasn't dead. Thank goodness. "You good?" Light spilled in from the opening the guard made in the wall, but it was dim at best. Not enough to see the big man well.

"Good, Kel. I'm good." He still held me, grip like iron. "Easy does," he repeated, concerned. "Don't wanna knock you out again."

"That was you?" No wonder my nose was pulped.

"Had to," he said. "You were about to...you know." He grimaced, face soured. "Could see your face."

Ah. *That* face. The one that meant Osiet Ros was getting off.

"You have to hit me so hard?" I tried to wriggle my nose. Ow. Stupid subconscious.

"Wouldn't go down, brother." Olly finally released my arms. I staggered against the web wall, legs almost giving now that he wasn't taking my weight. "Had to get a little rough."

"Well shit." No wonder — Olly's *a little rough* was like trying to fight a freight train. "Thanks for not killing me," *I think.*

"You got it," the big man smiled. "Now, need to catch you up. You been out."

"Yeah…" I trailed, looking back up at fug-face staring down at us. The spider hadn't moved, waiting to see how this would play out. Unnerving. "Who's your friend?"

"Iqa," Olly hooked his thumb over his shoulder. "He's aight." The spider twitched its mandibles, chittering a confirmation, then spreading the sharp pincers wide. I felt a happy vibration through the web wall now taking my weight.

"Is that supposed to be a smile?" It did absolutely nothing to make the spider look nice. Had the opposite effect, really, making its already fugly face look even more menacing.

"I think so," Olly shrugged. "Been real good company while you were out. Just looks super intimidating."

"Like someone else I know?" Couldn't help the jab.

"Hey now," Olly poked back. "You ain't winning any beauty pageants right now."

I cracked a grin, teeth wobbling as I did. Damnit, Olly.

Iqa, for his part, closed his jaws and cocked his head to the side, trying to cipher what the hell we were on about. I really hoped he didn't take offense at being called ugly. I doubted our humor translated well — hard enough for regular people to get.

"So," cutting to the chase, "sit rep."

"Prisoners, obviously."

"Obviously." I held up my shackled wrists.

"They're still debating. Been at it since..." Olly mimed punching me. "Ciacha's very persuasive, but the blue one keeps parading the dead kids." I grimaced. "They've got me working fields meanwhile, helping grow the shit they eat."

I shuddered — really didn't want to know, but had to ask. "What's that?"

"Lulu says it's a mix of my seats," Olly cocked his head and furrowed his brow, listening and trying to sort the science shit. "Why didn't you just say 'slime mold' to start with? It's gross, anyway."

"Better than the alternative." Relieved a bit by that. "Weapons?"

"No joy," Olly frowned. "All locked up. Iqa here keeps an eye on me in the camp though, makes sure no one mistakes me for food."

"I think you'd sort that pretty soon yourself."

"Prolly," he smiled. No *probably* about it. "But Iqa still shows me around. He's a good sort."

The spider must have understood we were talking about him — he rose a bit higher, basking in the complimentary tone. That seemed more important than the actual words spoken.

"How long til the party's over?" We didn't have time to fuck around, and that's exactly what I'd been doing.

"Couple days," Olly hedged. "I hope. You been out near two cycles of dark, however long those are." He paused, consulting his rider. "I haven't been able to check the gear. Had ninety-six hours when we got dug o ut."

Joy.

/10/

The *insurance policy* they'd saddled Olly with had a failsafe: weekly check-ins to make sure we weren't all dead — not that they cared — and reset the clock. We miss it. Kaboom. Any sign of being compromised. Kaboom. Ready to write us off. Kaboom.

Lots of kaboom.

"Should probably get going on that." I tried to take a step toward the door. Wasted enough time being hurt already.

"Roger that." Olly grabbed my arm, holding me upright. "But not now. You in no shape, for one."

I started to argue, but Olly held firm.

"'Sides," he cocked his head back at fugmo, "quittin' time. We're in for the night."

I eyed Iqa, rewebbing the opening he'd made in our cage. Olly could probably have forced him — no, that was stupid. No matter how desperate the situation. I got the feeling if we tried anything, the rest would *feel* it through the ever-present web and then it wouldn't really matter if the failsafe blew.

"Fine," I slumped myself to the wall. "Hurry up and wait it is."

"Ain't that the truth," Olly agreed, settling against the curving outer wall. "Gonna snag some Zs, brother."

Before I could even 'rar,' the big man was out. Sleep when you can.

I couldn't.

So I did what I always did when I couldn't sleep; I worked.

Gingerly, I got to my feet again, testing them in the dark. Less squishy than they'd been. The webbing had hardened while I slept, making sort of a cast. Whatever, it braced me, even if it was cumbersome. I could walk.

And box.

I'd already figured out my arms were okay — relatively. I mean, I didn't think they'd fall off if I hit something.

My nose, I couldn't do anything about, but that's why I had my guard up. High and tight, bob and weave. I ran through the drills my brother had beaten into me. I pulled at loose threads from the cell wall, wrapping them around my fists like tape. Bind and brace, keep the fist together.

Slowly through the night my footwork improved. Too slow for my taste, falling flat on my ass embarrassingly more than once. I couldn't even blame it on the restraints — I had just enough play, and it wasn't like I'd never trained with bands before.

My breath sharpened as my feet grew steady, beating the shit out of whatever enemy I could imagine. Thugs, punks, enemy combatants, fellow soldiers — anyone I'd thrown hands with.

Jab, cross. Jab, jab, cross. And again.

Jab, cross, step, hook. Press 'em til they fall.

Upper, upper, cross. Peekaboo, I see you.

Jab, jab, liver, hook. Shadow never saw it coming.

Necrobots, too, but that flowed differently in the sweet science.

Jab, jab, jab, guard, cross, upper, away — imagining the legs coming at me. Some stabbed, some shoved, some merely in the way as I wove under and through for the kill.

On and on through the night like this — clearing my mind, working the kinks, flushing pent-up adrenaline. I hurt like hell, but it was a good hurt. A working hurt. A living hurt.

"Forty-eight," I huffed. "Forty-nine," so close, "fifty," set finished.

"Shit man, you up all night?"

"Fifty-one," I went on. "Fifty-two," and done. I collapsed and rolled on my back.

"Why d'you always do two extra?" Olly'd woken up around number thirty but knew to keep his mouth shut.

"One for my brother," I wheezed. It'd been a long night. "And one for the Airborne Ranger in the sky." Who didn't come home.

I wondered for a second if they'd make some rook remember everything about me. Sure as hell doubted I'd be going home. Spiders, nukes, my own command...

"You have acquitted yourself well thus far," the thunder awoke uncharacteristically supportive.

"You've been pretty damn quiet tonight."

"What she saying?" I still wasn't sure Ros *was* a she. Or a he or an it or...whatever the Eshali were.

"The redistribution of your diminishing resources required much focus," was the answer floating before my face.

"Says I'm hungry," I cut to the chase. "Got anything to eat, Olly? They must've given you *something*."

"Nada on the chow," Olly shook his head. Weird to see him in the rider light. Couldn't make out expressions, only shapes moving all flittery. The motion sent motes flying — looking like a dog shaking

water off all slow-mo. "Got a bullet and a bit of candy bar
"

"I'll have some of the bar." We all carried rounds like that. But let's not go there.

"I know that's not how bullets work," Olly argued with Lulu, apparently. "Yes, I can," he went on, breaking me off a bite of the chocolate. "I just have to chomp on the primer...it will, too."

I wasn't getting in the middle of that. I was going to shut up and enjoy my Snicker snack — focusing carefully on not rearranging my teeth as I chewed.

That was one thing that hadn't healed up like the rest as I'd boxed.

Time enough for that later. Now, I turned my attention to the web wall and the guard's pincer-like leg undoing the door. Iqa poked his fugly head in, reaching for Olly — attaching his shackles to a lead line.

Seeing me upright and walking, Iqa chittered behind him, pulling back to let another spider reach a spindly green leg in to attach a strand of web to my own restraints. I was on work detail today.

"Nerix," Olly gestured toward mine by way of introduction. I guess they'd met.

My guard looked a lot happier than Iqa, strangely enough. He had a happy face tattooed on his back from the looks of things. Bright yellow-green all over with the black markings forming the grin once we got into the sunshine.

Crazy bastard was probably one hell of a fighter — I couldn't see any openings to slip in. Those green legs were spindly but left no gaps, and he walked with a swaggering step that reminded me nothing so much as a boxer's bob and weave — especially when the spider stepped side to side, nearly pulling me off balance. But not quite.

The fields our guards took us to weren't far from where we were kept — it *was* a tunnel. One of the many I'd seen diving back into the hillside as we spider-roped in, all covered in white webbing over the rocks. The webs spread out from the cave mouths and down into the valley studded with white sack lunches.

Further on, I saw the emaciated refugees feeding on the wriggling forms — barely able to eat their fill. Often not, as other guards pushed them off their sate. Spider soup line.

"There's not enough," I stated the obvious.

"No," Olly frowned. "Seen lots of 'em going at it like they did when we got here. Losers get ate, too."

"Good riddance." Sharp words floated across the scene, privation rampant in every direction I looked.

I ignored the callous dismissal of suffering. Maybe I could do something. Maybe I could help, for once, without the extreme violence.

"You said they're slime molds?" I knelt next to one of the smaller web sacs, not yet grown wriggly and plump.

"Lulu's talking science," the big man frowned, "but yeah, I think."

I wondered.

From where I knelt, I could feel the slightest pulse in the goo. Carefully, I encouraged it to fullness, imagining something like the bountiful fields Osiet Ros had flashed in counter to the destruction.

"Kel," Olly fretted. Our guards looked on, seemingly uncertain what was happening.

A thrum swept through the field, swelling the webs to bursting — sending the surrounding spiders into a frenzy as the slime fields suddenly quickened to excess, triggering the prey drive of a hundred hunters all at once.

"Kellan!" I felt screeching spider legs through the webs beneath my feet as the masses closed in, this near-fallow field now ripened.

I went flying through the air, yanked by my wrists and landed pinned against a rock face — my guard in my face. He no longer looked happy as he shoved me above the feeding fracas.

Olly landed next to me up top while Iqa and Nerix kept the flood tide at bay. Or tried to.

"What'd you do?"

"Fed them," I said simply, taking in the writhing mass of chitinous bodies. The scope was hardly imaginable. Giant spiders the size of school buses mixed with those the size of dogs — and likely smaller, but I couldn't distinguish them as easily.

What I did see, though, was a blessing.

"You got your mirror?" I nodded subtly up at the canyon rim as the big man looked up at me from the frenzy. He nodded back, reaching to his chest.

"One gets you two?" he asked as he casually slipped the thin bit of polished metal from a tiny Velcro pouch dead center of his chest, mimicking a stretch and scratch.

"One gets you two," I confirmed, waiting for the 'one' in question to flash again.

It came. Olly flashed twice.

"And two gets you three." I waited for confirmation.

Hot damn. We had a friend.

/11/

The question was how to talk to our friend. The frenzy from the rampant growth stunt I'd pulled had only lasted a few minutes — Nerix settled *that* real quick.

Side note: Don't fuck with Nerix. He wasn't taking anyone's shit and put the mob down with broken legs, severed limbs, and more than a few bashed heads. My assessment had been right — helluva fighter. He danced on two of his legs while four more laid into nearby targets and the last two slung gobby web-bullets at any not in range. Gummed 'em right up.

I hadn't needed Olly's translation to make out the chittery curses flying left and right — atmospheric bordering on fucking punctuation — all strung together with an ode to the violence of action sung along the web. But it was nice to have confirmation.

"Knew some Brits once, SAS," Olly reminisced as we'd watched the melee dying down. "F-this, ya bloody C- that. Nerix would'a fit right in."

Now we stood with the council again in their little circle, deciding our fate — what else was new? At least these pricks were going to kill us to our face.

At least, I assumed they were going to execute us. We'd killed hundreds — if not thousands — of their kind. We provided a convenient someone to hang that nest's destruction on — appeasing hard-liners like Saizsir. *And* we'd just caused a minor riot while captive — too dangerous. Three strikes.

Our bosses had only needed one. And most of those were fabricated, like my jacket.

It was going badly for our side, overall. Brass needed more bodies for the Eshali to ride — more weapons. The whole problem hadn't been made public, of course. No. Top secret. Hush hush.

I only found out about it when I received a damning envelope under my door — a door MPs beat down not too long after.

It'd been enough.

Enough to charge me with espionage. Enough to railroad me through a kangaroo court-martial. Enough to condemn me to death.

Enough for me to let them do it, too.

If only so I could do right by Gerald.

That trial had been far less... symphonic, shall we say? Just a bunch of gaveling and a litany of falsehoods ushering my fate along. This one was like a night at the opera.

The elder, white-carapaced spider led things off with an overture followed by other bits from the Looney Tunes intro I remembered as a kid on Saturday mornings. Ciacha pled our case. Sapphire rebutted. Others chimed in here and there.

I wasn't so much listening as feeling the music of the proceedings. They weren't exactly forming full words for me now — not like the first night we'd been brought in. Probably hallucinated that — blood loss will fuck you over.

Hard.

But I still got the gist of it.

"Ready when you say, Kel," Olly leaned in to whisper. "This don't look good."

It didn't, but I wasn't healed enough for a brawl, and I still had one trick up my sleeve.

"Finally, you listen to reason." The delighted words floated in the back of my brain, showing me choice orbital munitions for varying degrees of decimation.

"No," I squashed the bloodlust. Loud enough the council halted what was being said... strummed. Whatever it was they did to make the music.

I felt a puzzled look from Olly, and somehow, the thunder in my heart shared the sentiment. It was a long shot, but better than nothing.

"If you kill us," I strode forward, my tone clear, "you die." I turned the circle, making sure I had the attention of all present. "Every last one of you."

I felt the rage through the web at my feet, heard the mad chittering of the onlookers as their leader tried to assert authority. Their hatred filled my bones. Only Ciacha looked the slightest bit concerned for my head — the rest called for it in a sack.

"Kel?" Olly flexed in his bindings, working them ever looser. He could have slipped them with his bootstraps if he wanted to, but he'd been trying not to rile our captors up. And they hadn't hurt us, yet. That might've been changing.

"You threaten us?" the bleached white elder locked eight cold eyes on me. I guess I hadn't been hallucinating. Or this message was just particularly clear.

"No threats." I stood my ground and held up two fingers and a thumb. "Three ways it will come to pass should we die."

"A prophecy that cannot be wrong," Ros flashed the mirthful letters, thinking what I was thinking.

"One," I started the countdown, lowering my thumb, "the stars will fall again upon our deaths."

"Shall I give them a taste?" Ros ached to demonstrate — I could feel the lust for destruction as the Eshali took aim from orbit.

"Second," I went on, touching my pointer finger. "Should we die, we will be unable to stop our weapons from detonating — which they will without intervention." Unease rippled through the web.

"Lastly," I flipped them off for good measure. "Without our aid, the Avispa will enslave or eradicate any of your people who remain after those first two calamities."

The council tensed, unsure what to do now that I'd made it a standoff — kill us and take their chances with the rocks and nuke and wasps. Or listen.

"I'm a dead man any way you slice it," I grinned, bravado on full blast. "Care to join me?"

Deep inside, peals of thunder laughed with gleeful abandon.

The council spiders didn't find the situation nearly as funny as Osiet Ros did — or as I did — not sharing our morbid sense of humor. But it gave them pause as the violent rage of the web's song quelled to a dull throb.

"You insignificant flesh bags," Saizsir lit in, shaking in agitation barely contained. *"See how the barbarians threaten? A desperate bluff, no doubt. They cannot be*

trusted. Remove their heads and the threat along with them."

"It feels no idle threat," a mirrored spider spoke for the first time. Elegant chords delicately wove into the stern rondo of the sapphire spider. *"My agents confirmed their capacity, and appetite, for destruction."* Agents? Their spymaster? Thoughts for later.

"Look," I leveled with them. "You know you're fucked — you're on the run, desperately outmatched by your enemy, barely able to feed your swelling numbers. We're just as fucked. But we can help each other." Stick and carrot.

"Sticks work better when shown, not said," Osiet Ros counseled in throaty rumble behind speckled words.

I preferred the bounty side of my gift, if I'm honest. It felt good to create for once, not destroy. To help.

"To help these monsters feast on your own," thunder spat.

"Are we going to make this work, or not?" I looked around the circle of spiders. Ciacha seemed pleased while Saizsir fumed. The mirrored, slinking spider stroked a leg on the web beneath the leader — a word in private.

"Disarm your weapons," the white spider leading the refugees — whose name I never caught — sent through the web. *"A sign of good faith."*

Shit. I shot a glance toward Olly.

"Can you?" Lulu'd had him tinkering with the nuke pack since first deployment — a waste to let all that energy go unused — but I didn't know if he could disarm the failsafe without the codes from command.

"Give it a shot," Olly shrugged. "Rather not blow up myself."

"We can do that," I turned back to the elder. "A sign of good faith," I repeated, holding his eight eyes with mine, holding up my shackling webs.

Mirth filled the eight black eyes of the snowy elder, bleached with age. It reached one long leg toward me, briefly pausing over the tensile strands —considering — before touching the center of my chest.

"You press your luck, manling," the elder spoke directly with me — filling my head with a symphony of one. *"And amuse me,"* it laughed. *"You are correct in your assessments — we are badly losing — and I am inclined to bring you to our cause,"* it paused to spare a glance at the hard-liners in the group who'd clenched their spinnerets, *"but I cannot yet. Too many resist still."*

"Then we will make them listen," I spoke low, allowing the vibrations to travel up the enormous leg pressed uncomfortably against my chest. The sensation was ethereal — plenty of necrobots had gotten in close quarters before, but never had I felt the music from contact. This elder's song filled me with the life lived, showing me flashes of the spider's past, the complex emotions intricately layered in time. I even saw, very briefly, a time before the Avispa had enslaved their kind. I was in awe of just how much could be conveyed by their song — now that I knew to listen.

"We must," it agreed, drawing back the finely haired leg.

It seemed we had more allies among the spiders than just Ciacha.

"Bring their weapons," it commanded sharply to nearby spiders. *"Try anything and perish,"* it warned — not just show for the hard-liners either. Smiling-Jack Nerix and fug-face Iqa pressed closer to me and Olly, reminding us of their presence.

Something felt off, but I pushed it to the back of my mind. Probably just the whole fucked up situation.

"As it is always merely the wind," sarcasm dripped from the murmured thunder.

What was Ros on about?

The spiders parted in a vibrato of action, allowing the guards bearing our weapons to pass through. Synchronized by the shared harmonics, each adding their song to the whole — a persistent track in the back of my mind.

Except...

Cautiously, I leaned back against Nerix's leg, trying not to draw attention.

Silence.

Shit.

The laughing green spider was Songless.

/12/

"*...stack the bodies of Songless...*" I recalled Ciacha exhorting the sapphire Saizsir. It's what they called the necrobots — Songless.

And my guard had no song. Not like I'd just felt from the elder spider's touch. Not like I'd felt riding Ciacha's back so long — not knowing what it was at the time. Not until I'd heard her impassioned plea to the council. Until I'd been immersed in their symphony.

Snippets like static burst up my spine as I looked to the giant spider looming above me — poised to strike at any moment should I step out of line. Nerix shook his head, mandibles quivering. One eye twitched, then another, as if wracked with a spasm.

"The Avispa claim another," Osiet Ros rumbled, motes shaping the words before swirling into others.

"The impregnated larva fights the spider for control, ceasing the music."

"Songless," I whispered as I felt it stop, replaced instead by the tell-tale hiss I was used to from the necrobots.

I wasn't the only one to hear the guard's song cease. Iqa locked eyes on his partner, terrible notes sprung from the spider — screeching notes of horror sawed across violin strings. The brown giant reared to confront the new threat, throwing Olly to the side. I dove after the big man before the new necrobot could skewer my unguarded back.

Around us, chaos bloomed as the massive ogre-faced spider squared off against the agile, grinning green. Those surrounding the council pressed close to see what was the matter while the council itself tried to maintain calm and order.

"What happened?" Olly righted himself, coming to my side while keeping low.

"Nerix went necrobot." I tried to put the pieces together myself. "What Ros said."

"Damnit all," Olly spat. "We need to help," he started into the fight.

"Olly, wait..." Too late.

The big man roared as he went for Nerix's leg — trying to help Iqa put the green spider on its back — only to be rewarded with a stout round-kick from the skilled fighter. After seeing how easily the smiling spider had put the riot down, I hoped I'd never have to fight him.

Well fuck. Embrace the suck.

I jumped in with Olly as he rounded Nerix's blind side while I hopped up on Iqa's back as the two spiders grappled. Without my knuckle busters my strikes needed to be far more surgical — aimed at joints and other weak spots — and those tended to be higher than I could reach.

Unless I leaped from the back of a giant...

...and landed on a thrashing green rage monster.

Not the smartest thing I've ever done — far from it — but it's what I did. I kicked my boot toe in the gaps between the spider's legs and body as I landed, causing not-Nerix to jerk and stumble, allowing Iqa to gain advantage. My fingers found another gap and hooked in for the ride.

Olly swung while I rode, knocking a back leg out with a loud CRACK — breaking the sharp stabbing tip, leaving only the gushing stub the necrobot tried to scrabble back on. The fugly guard pressed, toppling the green spider on its back and throwing his weight into pinning the necrobot.

I braced, hanging on for dear life as the green husk collapsed in the dust of this wretched world. The dead spider thrashed as Iqa pressed close — if spiders could cry, the guard would be bawling, I felt.

Sorrow filled Iqa's song as the spider came into close contact with the remains of Nerix, pleading for it not to be so. Disbelief and shock ascended into the melody as the green spider plunged one wicked sharp leg deep into Iqa's side.

"NO!" Olly bellowed in rage, snapping the offending limb clean off with one strike.

I landed a punch of my own. Surgical. Straight to the base of the head where it met the thorax — severing it cleanly from the body.

Wish I hadn't.

I don't regret killing him — fucker needed killing and I'm sure Nerix wouldn't have wanted his body used to kill those he'd sworn to protect. Whoever else he'd been, he'd been a soldier. That's all I needed to know.

The thing that writhed and wriggled its way from Nerix's corpse wasn't.

It was evil. And hella disgusting — long, translucent flesh, nearly limpid, bathed in the gouting purple viscera of the fallen as it emerged from the wound. The wormlike thing turned on me — I swore it was glaring at me, lumps of flesh pinched like angry eyebrows — and unleashed a nasty, piercing screech from pinholes along its body.

"Kill it, squash it, grind its oily flesh to goo and light it aflame," peals of thunder enjoined as the creature squirmed toward the hole it had made in Iqa's side.

Olly beat me to it, popping the parasite in his massive grip. Slow to anger and gentle to a fault, his face transformed into a rictus snarl as he thoroughly squashed the bug.

I'd been so focused on our fight, I hadn't noticed the chaos around us as spider fought spider — the once harmonious symphony discordant and stilted...but that wasn't the worst. A horrible buzz rose above the tattered melody.

"The Avispa come," maniacal letters glimmered over the scene of utter carnage.

In all our trips through, I'd never seen one of the Avispa in the flesh — only their necrobot foot soldiers — but anything that buzzed like that could fuck right off.

"We got incoming," I called over to the enraged Olly, still taking the pre-pupescent evil apart. "Up top."

Our eyes snapped to the ridge line — nothing yet, but the buzz grew louder. There, too, I could see the guards fighting amongst themselves. Something else moved as well, I thought.

"Insidious," Ros observed. "The seeds of destruction laid in their own kind."

"Lulu's saying they're sleepers." Olly yanked the green leg piercing Iqa's side out of the spider, slinging his friend's ichor off his improvised weapon. "Terrorists."

"Ros, too." I looked for my own stabby bit of spider or anything really I could use.

"You've an entire sky to call down upon your enemies," Osiet Ros tempted, showing me the de-orbiting trajectories of a thousand rocks.

I settled for cracking off a bit of green carapace instead — lashing it to my arm as a shield with a bit of sticky web churned up in the struggle. I wanted to strap bits on my chest and back as well — looked like I was about to be getting up close and real personal — but was interrupted by the wispy spider flick-flacking its way toward us, all legs and haste.

The sticky webs that hindered my own footing — it was like trying to walk on wet cement — seemed not to bother this cartwheeling spider as it skimmed along the surface.

Friend or foe? No way to tell unless I either got close enough to hear their song — or lack thereof — or two, they attacked — and even then, they might just be a pissed-off spider, not a necrobot. Both options sucked.

No time to dwell on it as the spider lunged straight for me at top speed — barely skidding to a halt, one leg raised for a strike, as I braced and raised my guard.

The leg swung, knife edge cutting straight down the middle — aimed to split my head wide open. Except, instead of my head, it sliced my cuffs.

So friend-spider? No further signs of aggression, and it began chittering faster than it'd spun.

"He says to come with him," Olly from the side, lowering his green spear. He'd already brute-forced his binds somewhere along the way, beast that he is. "Yasha's gathering survivors. And has our weapons," he grinned at this last.

I didn't know which one Yasha was, but if they were giving us our gear back, I liked them. Maybe that was the elder's name — I'd never caught it, even in the song. He seemed inclined to peace between us.

I didn't have time to ask as a necrobot joined the chat, crashing down where the little flick-flack spider stood with a hiss and a squish. Large and mottled-red, the dead spider rose to strike.

I rolled to the side — prying my feet out of the wet cement as best I could — coming up with my shield braced for the impact that soon came. I hadn't gotten very far in my roll, so it wasn't hard for the necrobot to deliver a blunt swat after the first strike missed.

While I had its attention, though, Olly came in hot from the opposite side, jabbing Nerix's leg-spear into our assailant's abdomen and taking a spurt of viscera to the face. The red husk's legs collapsed — animate force bleeding out — curling up under itself and causing it to roll over onto the big man.

Even dead — again — the assholes kept coming.

Olly's luck held, though, as another walking corpse diverted the death roll of the spasming necrobot.

"Iqa!" Olly's face lit up, seeing his friend lived.

The ogre-faced guard wasn't dead after all, but it didn't look good. He walked on four legs — the two around the stab wound refused to work, curling close against him. Another leg from opposite the wound looked to be holding pressure on the gusher, loosely packed with webs. Hell of a field triage. With the last leg, one in the front, he shoved the necrobot clear as it thrashed, unable to right itself.

Olly finished it off, crunching the necrobot's head with his boot before seeing to Iqa — no squirmer popped out to say hi this time. The big man checked the wound, practiced farm hand going over the spider's side. "You got any more webs?"

The guard spider winced and his spinnerets glistened, dribbling white fluid, which he spun out gingerly with his back leg. Olly took them and began repacking the wound, his face smeared purple with blood as he worked.

During the triage, I pulled security — borrowing Olly's spear to go with my shield. The refugee camp looked a mess. Shambles — the symphonic webbing broken in a thousand places, ruining the harmonies, destroying any sense of cohesion the spiders had forged. The whole cluster was in disarray — exactly as the enemy had wanted.

"Iqa says we should make our way to Yasha," Olly relayed. "Like the little guy said." It hadn't ended well for the acrobatic little spider, getting caught unawares like that. But at least the message got through.

"Does he know where this Yasha is? Who are they?" I looked between Olly and Iqa, waiting to hear something from the guard myself, but his song was too weak, relying on the chittery pidgin Lulu translated for Olly.

"The shiny one at the council," he translated. Their spymaster, if I guessed right. "Second in command." Didn't like the sound of that. Something must've happened to the old guy, which sucked because I felt we were making progress.

Ifs and buts can suck my nuts, though. Nothing's ever ideal — gotta deal with what's real.

"How eloquently put," Ros chimed in.

"I haven't decided if you're exactly real yourself," I shot back. "Maybe we're all just crazy."

"Have to be," Olly grinned, helping take some of Iqa's weight as the big brown rose. "That's a lad," he told the spider. "Knew you were too ugly to die."

Olly said it, not me. Friends get to call you a steaming turd sack to your face and laugh it off, like Iqa did — I guess he was laughing. There was some sort of spasming, and I heard air moving.

"So, where we going?" We'd gotten side-tracked.

"That way," Olly nodded in the direction the dead messenger came from. Probably wasn't more than a kid himself. Stop. Focus.

"How the hell we going to get his ass up that hill?"

"We walk." Leave it to Olly to be patently practical.

"We walk," I echoed as the distant buzz grew louder. So, too, did the thunder in my heart.

Part 3: Long Walk, Short Fuse

/13/

"Leave him. He drags you down," my rider advised, writing on the canyon wall.

"Never leave a soldier behind," I insisted. Somehow we'd hauled the giant spider's ass nearly a klick through the shit — encountering a decreasing number of necrobots along the way. Most of which we avoided, letting the other spiders handle their business.

"He is the enemy." Slightly larger letters for 'enemy,' angrier too.

"Not right now, he's not." Iqa'd handled himself, stiff-arming attackers come close as Olly or I took them down, quick and efficient as we could. Needed to get Olly his railgun before flying death from above showed up — plus, there was that whole kaboom factor. And I really wanted my knuckle busters — felt naked without my weapon.

"Your weapon is everywhere," Osiet drew my eyes to the sky with floating words. The alien sky. On an alien planet. Populated by giant fucking spiders and — presumably — giant wasps, too.

The planet spun too fast for my taste. You wouldn't think it'd be something you noticed, but I sure did. And rings streaked across the greenish sky that just weren't right.

Back home, I used to look up at the sky on missions and think how it was the same sky as home, just looking down over some righteous shit going down on the other side of the world.

This sky was anything but comforting — bearing absolutely no resemblance to the blues and grays and reds and oranges and purples of home — and it was especially discomforting as I saw black dots against the green sky resolve into the source of the incessant buzz we'd been hearing.

"Where is she?" The little whippersnapper had come from this direction, but I saw no place for a giant-ass spider to hide. The ground rumbled, I stumbled — losing my feet as the hillside on which we stood gave way.

I lurched, grabbing onto the ground-covering webs as they turned vertical. Olly grabbed hold of Iqa's leg with one hand as the giant brown held firm to the shifting terrain. From each side, I saw two shimmering forms dart in quick, bladed legs to our throats.

The one on Olly also covered Iqa, wrapping hind legs around the brown's neck and what working legs he had, restricting his movement. I'd never gotten into MMA — sticking to the sweet science — but damn, that looked lethal.

"*Stay,*" the web shrilled — a harsh vibrato sung through the thread in my hand.

The blades held — not quite drawing blood, but I felt *something* wet at my throat.

"Toxin," Osiet floated the word, writing a sickly green. Great. Instant death or just paralysis. Neither a great option.

"The latter, so they may feast upon your entrails as you yet breathe," the words shifted. "Live prey is preferred." I shivered. Hopefully, these were friends.

Very close friends, as the sequined spider shoved its face into mine — black eyes examining me closely. My reflection nearly cringed myriad times under their glare — don't blink.

"Olly," to the side. "Down." Reflexively, he'd grabbed the knife leg, same as me — though while I was trying to keep death from my throat, Olly's grip verged on cracking the mirrored carapace. "I think we found Yasha."

"*Where is the young one?*" I squeezed my eyes shut — always taking the blame for those I couldn't save.

"Songless got him," I kept my voice level.

The spider at my throat looked to Iqa — confirmation, suspicion, I wasn't sure which. His own song had been weak since the gut wound. The brown ogre chittered something in the pidgin, signing it with a twitch of a rear leg.

I guess that was enough.

As quick as they'd appeared, the assassins vanished back into the web — concealed by darkness and their mirrored reflections. Ninja spiders. Damn. I hoped those never turned necrobot.

"*We can never be too careful.*" Another mirror gleamed in the darkness below — moving as it spoke for the first time, refracting the dim light.

"Yasha?" I assumed as I dangled from strands of the wall.

"*Come,*" it turned, beckoning us deeper. "*Your friends wait.*"

"Friends?" I thought we were here for weapons.

"Suck my fucking dick," a voice I didn't expect screamed. Totally *not* who I thought it'd be.

"Sounds like Doc," Olly drawled. "I'd have bet Javier."

I thought it'd be Luna, too. The spook got around.

"Señor," there he was, "It'd go a long way to good faith."

"You can stick your faith up your butt, amigo," Doc wasn't happy. "I ain't healing one of *them*," he spat. "Don't know if I even could."

"Maybe I c..." a third voice got cut off.

"NO!"

At least Luna and Doc agreed on something.

"Who was *that*?" Olly was as confused as I was by the third.

"Guess we better find out." I started picking my way down the web. "Can we get a fast rope?" I grumbled for a little gravity assist. Always hated the damn cargo net.

"Could just let go," Olly offered, looking down into the dark. Oh, how I wanted to sometimes.

"Don't think my legs could take it, big man." They were pulped enough — but maybe Doc could do something about that. And the face. "But if you're in a rush..."

"I'm good." Olly'd transferred from Iqa's leg to the web beside, letting the big brown go first. Didn't blame him, wouldn't want to be under that gravity assist.

Iqa, for his part, did fast rope. The bastard. Olly and I exchanged glances.

"You asked," he offered me first.

"Don't mind if I do." I side-scrabbled over to the attach point — then leapt, grabbing hold. No gloves, but if the web burned, Doc could fix that, I figured. Wasn't so bad without a pack, definitely better than jumping the gun — glad to ditch that when we got fresh meat.

The webbed walls passed in a blur as the bottom came to meet my feet. I tucked in a roll and cleared the landing — Olly dropping with a thud soon after. Both feet planted — solid guy. Yasha had vanished in the darkness, leaving us with Iqa and our squad mates.

"Subtle, Bostock," Doc muttered, ever blunt. "I'm not healing those clodhoppers if you busted 'em being stupid." Great bedside manner, our medic — baseball coach before he got saddled with a rider who could heal. Walk it off.

"Roger," Olly reflexively replied. "Help my friend, though?" He hooked his thumb over at Iqa, limping along the side of the cavern opening at the base of the funnel web.

Doc eyed the spider in disgust. "Can't do it. Won't do it," he huffed. "No way in hell."

"He saved my life," Olly leveled with the medic, his voice flat. "More than once."

Doc pursed his lips. That changed things. "Fine," he grumbled, spitting a wad of chaw. "Give it a shot. No promises." He eyed Olly as he hesitantly approached the wounded spider. You don't leave a brother hanging.

Guilt stabbed. Had he been able to save any of the others? Had I been their death or had the swarming necrobots — something I'd avoided thinking about, but now it stared me in the face.

"Good to see you, brother," Luna clapped a hand on my shoulder. Nothing else need be said; I could breathe again. We were good.

"Who's that?" I still didn't recognize the voice cut off earlier, piping up over the healing chant floating our way. Hard to tell who talked as the doc's voice rose in the dead tongue.

The hole was dark, and the rider-sight hadn't kicked in — or, rather, I hadn't turned it on. When I did, I saw the outline of a soldier sitting on a bucket, leaning on an impact driver — one hand wrapped around the haft, the other missing. Bandages covered his eyes.

"That you, Leland?" I could tell Olly grinned just from his voice, ever the earnest one. One of the things I liked about the big man: you knew exactly where you stood with him. Not a hint of subterfuge. "Holy shit, brother, glad Doc could patch you up. Kel, look..."

"Blaese! You son of a..." Guess he wasn't happy to — well I guess he couldn't see me. He tried, though, ripping at his covered eyes.

"Puta madre," Luna swore, flowing into a binding chant. Archaic script flowed from his mouth in the rider-sight, wrapping around the maimed soldier's head — fixing the gauze in place. That was new.

"You son of a bitch," Leland tore at his eyes. "I'll kill him. I'll kill him!" He lurched up from the bucket seat, lashing out with the driver handle as he stumbled forward. "Where is he..."

"Whoa, man, easy." Olly grabbed the hammer haft in one hand, carefully gripping Leland with the other. "What's the deal?"

"What's the deal!? WHAT'S THE DEAL!!?" Pure hatred filled his voice as Leland turned his covered glare on Olly — as if trying to burn a hole through the wrappings and into the big man. The sheer intensity of it...the white cloth started smoking. "He dropped the fucking sky on us!" Leland flung his arm back at the bucket. "*That's* the deal."

"Dropped one on me, too," Olly said calmly. "Most of a mountain, too," he actually laughed. "But Major made him do it."

I kept my mouth shut.

"You'd know that better than most," Olly reasoned, nodding toward Leland's stub.

"That's not what..." The angry, confused soldier deflated.

"...the major said?" Olly finished the thought.

Leland's face fell flat, his body slackening in Olly's grip. The snarl curling his lip lost its rictus, his shoulders slumped from their coiled violence, his fiery rage abated. "Sorry," he said, but there was no forgiveness.

"S'alright." The major had been cultivating that rep among the men since I'd been assigned. Kept everyone at a distance. Kept them on their toes. I was the unit killer. Easy to hate me, not him.

Not like it wasn't earned. *I* hadn't done it, but whoever'd got Osiet before me had.

"What's with the eyes?" I changed the subject. Last I saw, he'd only hurt one. "And the chanting." Luna had stopped once Leland had quit clawing his face — the glowing coils of dead letters stopped along with it. I'd never actually seen the magic, our abilities — whatever it was the Eshali gave us — at work before. Just the results.

"Our boy here is a late bloomer," Luna explained nothing.

"Before the *incident*," Leland's voice caught at the word, hesitating. "I didn't have anything *special*," he backtracked a bit. "Just stronger, faster, couldn't..." *cause an apocalypse,* I wanted to fill in. "So they stuck me in the squad with a gun and told me to shoot shit."

I thought we'd all gotten something — some just didn't want to say what, some was classified. Left hand right hand shit — but I guess not.

"As you have ranks, so, too, do we," Osiet added context to the scene in rider-sight. "Some aid in only the most basic ways, while I..." the thunder trailed off — promises of unfathomable destruction hanging like favored rocks in orbit.

"He blows shit up if he looks at it," Doc bluntly summed it up as he came back to the group — wiping his hands on his BDUs. They'd been stained purple. "Or fixes it," he added with a shrug. "Don't know which till he does it. Nearly took my face off after I patched him up."

"Some patch job," Leland growled. "You just rubbed some dirt on it!"

"It worked, didn't it?" Doc leaned against the wall and slipped down to the ground. Seemed spent. I'd give him a minute before I asked about the nose — who knew what baseball fix he'd give it. "You can see, just shouldn't."

"How's he doing?" Olly asked after Iqa.

"Did what I could — which wasn't much — but I think it'll be fine," Doc leaned his head back and shut his eyes.

"*You did well,*" the walls sang. "*He rests now. We thank you.*" What little light there had been gathered now, reflecting off the silvery scales of the mirrored spider as it approached. Behind the spymaster came a familiar silhouette.

"Ciacha!"

"What's a Ciacha?" Luna looked a bit on edge, unsure about so many spiders coming so close despite his playing peacemaker. I saw him itch the pouch he kept his destruct-o-tiles in.

"It's a dance." Glad I wasn't the only one whose brain immediately went there.

"She's Ciacha," Olly clarified. "That's her name."

"They have names?" Doc's ignorance was showing.

"'Course they do," Olly grinned. "How else you tell 'em apart?"

"I don't."

"Well, that's Ciacha," Olly pointed to our friend with the orange patches. "Yasha, I think," pointing out the silvered spider. "I hear she's in charge around here. And Iqa's the big one you fixed up."

"More war-makers!" Ciacha's song was delighted. *"The Songless shall wither and the Winged-ones will pay!"* She reared high, chittering loudly in praise.

Reflexively, everyone but me and Olly crouched and raised guard — even Leland, and he was damn well blind. Muscle memory was one thing, but these were allies now — not hostiles.

"They understand not the spider-song," Ros illuminated in thunder.

"Translation, Olly," I prompted. I'd started taking understanding them for granted, while Luna and the rest probably didn't have a damn clue what was going on. No wonder their sphincters were clenched so tight.

"You understand them, big man?" Luna spared a glance for Olly, slowly pulling his hand away from the tile pouch.

"Lulu translates a bit for me, but I'm starting to pick it up." Maybe he'd felt the song like I had. "She said 'More war-makers,' that's what she calls us." He left out the times she called us biting-food, thank goodness.

"You got presents for us?" I'd spotted the gear sacs slung on Ciacha's back as she'd come down the corridor behind Yasha.

"I have your war tools, yes," Olly translated as the spider unraveled the webbing. "You walk again," Ciacha addressed me. "Good to fight side by side once more."

"Betray our trust," Yasha warned as we went for our gear, *"and perish most heinously."*

"Not sure we'll have time for all that," Olly blanched, flipping open the failsafe.

Red wasn't a good color.

The darkness made it worse, magnifying the ominous light bathing Olly's face, picked up by Yasha's mirrors as she moved to see and thrown throughout the room, casting everything in unspilled blood.

"At least it's not..." Luna began to say 'blinking' when the light flickered off.

And on again.

"Had to jinx it," Olly put in.

"Ay dios mio," he turned sharply, "puta mierda…" and trailed off from there faster than I could catch.

"What's that mean?"

"Shh, I'm counting," the big man said.

"Don't hurt yourself, Bostock." Doc had a gift for being reflexively ass-holeish — probably sass the reaper himself when his time's up.

Thirty seconds. One minute. I held my breath.

"How long…" I broke the silence as the light blinked again.

Olly bit his lip and listened to Lulu. "Siiiiixty-four minutes, aaaand twelve seconds…eleven…ten…"

"We get the picture," I grumbled. "Not long."

"It's hunting for signal," Luna weighed in. "It'll try again."

"And then the countdown starts."

"Can Lulu turn it off?" We needed a plan.

Olly shook his head.

"Could break it," Luna went for a tile at his belt. " *Malcriado de mierda…*"

"Would the railgun still work?" Gotta cover all the angles.

Again, a headshake. Real wordy, our Olly.

"What's that matter? Just break the damn thing before it blows," Doc shot off. "Better yet, leave it while we high tail it. Let it take care of our," he nodded slightly upward, "problems."

The spiders who'd been staying out of our spirited discussion — I wasn't sure if they weren't keeping up with the rapid-fire or were simply waiting — joined in.

"Disarm or die," Yasha, straight to the point — bladed leg at the doc's throat. Faster than thought. *"You gave your word,"* she turned her head toward me. Words or not, they'd read the tone.

"We will, we will," I tried to defuse the situation before *it* went nuclear. "We can't disarm..." Yasha twitched, readying a strike. "...but we can break it." I clarified.

"Then break *it,"* Yasha didn't let off her point.

"On it," Luna knelt by the pack, taking out a clay tile — the dead tongue was almost at his lips.

"Not yet," I locked eyes with the mirrored, holding her gaze, my tone even. As rational and non-threatening as I could make it.

"Por que no?" Technically, Luna out-ranked me, but he didn't have all the facts, so I risked the interruption. Luckily, Javier's not an ass and could listen to his people.

"Any of you fuckers got anything else that can take out air support?" I risked a glance at the guys.

"You do," Osiet Ros, ever tempting me with sweet words of violence.

"I could..." Leland ventured.

"No," I said. Luna and Doc said. Even Olly said. None of us wanted to risk it.

"Barring walking apocalypses," I included myself, "Olly's railgun is *it*, and we've got bogeys inbound." How long had we been chatting? "If they aren't already here." I looked back at Yasha. She'd know.

"The Winged-ones breached the top layer minutes ago," Yasha acknowledged. I figured she'd have her thumb — so to speak — on the pulse of things.

"They've breached," I translated before Olly could — damn, didn't want to let that on. "Top layer of..." I couldn't remember how many.

"Three," Olly filled in. "By my count, at least." Yasha neither confirmed nor denied.

"Right, so two until this entire refugee camp is swarmed, and *that*," I hooked my thumb at the red glow, "is our only bug spray." The light blinked again. Perfect timing.

"Perfecto," Luna took back command. "Backward attack until target neutralized, objective reached, or we blow up. Easy, no?" He gave a quick smile.

Easy. Sure.

/14/

No one likes a quitter — even quitters don't like quitters — that's why Rangers never say retreat. It's a backward attack — sometimes bass-ackward if it's FUBARred enough.

I don't think they've come up with an acronym for this shit yet.

"Arrest them!" And now it was worse. Saizsir's glimmering sapphire carapace blocked the path through the rocks Yasha had led us to. The big blue asshole reared four legs high, ready to strike down as big brown fuglies — they could be Iqa's twins — flanked us on the rock faces to either side, moving in. More stood ready behind.

"Remove yourself from our path," Yasha commanded as Olly and I took action — the doom tube's hopper

whirred to comforting life. Strangely, I'd missed that sound — and the one that followed.

WHUFWHUFWHUFskittercrumble as the rounds cracked the ground — halting the advancing guards.

"I think you missed, big man." Doc stuck close to Leland at the rear. The blinded soldier leaned on the driver haft like a staff — bucket slung across his shoulder. I never asked what was in there, but I could guess. Never leave anyone behind.

"Just warning 'em," Olly grinned. "Still friendlies."

"Violent friends," Luna chimed in, pulling some tiles.

"Still getting to know each other." I had a bad feeling. "That guy kinda sucks."

"We ain't got time for this, just kill the damn bugs." Doc hadn't quite accepted our *alliance* with the rebels.

The former ball player hurled a grenade at the sapphire. Damn good arm — cleared us and placed it right in the middle of the chest — but the spider batted it up and over the ridge.

"You see!" Saizsir shuddered at the enhanced explosion as the grenade detonated. *"Barbarians! There is no doubt they killed Leuc."*

"Who's Leuc?" Shoulder to shoulder with Olly, my knuckle busters charged — didn't quite make a sound, but they tingled. Also comforting.

Olly's answer was drowned out in the flood of Yasha's scream. I'd never seen the spy mistress as anything but perfectly composed, but the discordant noise that ripped from her as she leapt at Saizsir told me all I needed to know.

"Their leader's dead." So was any hope of an alliance — especially if Saizsir was shoving blame at us. "Fuck."

Saizsir swatted Yasha with a thick leg, knocking her into the rock face. *"Traitor! She sides with the enemy,"* he flung the accusation. Political theater. God damn, I was tired of that kind of shit. Every-damn-where I went, there it was.

"We gotta go," Luna picked up the read, scanning for a way out.

Yasha screamed again and came back at Saizsir with knives drawn — bringing sharp legs, dripping with paralytic toxin, forward as she lunged. The mirror spider buried one in a sapphire leg, but the size difference between the two was overwhelming, and Saizsir swatted her away again.

Olly launched a volley as the guards tried to pounce on Yasha, still not aiming for the kill — we hadn't been directly attacked yet, and Olly wouldn't be the aggressor. Damn, did I wish a fucker would, though.

Doc had no such compunction, flinging another incendiary dead at the giant brown spiders.

These did not have the reflexes of their insurgent leader and took the full brunt of the fireball. The flaming mix clung to their carapace, cracking and popping as their viscera boiled. Thankfully, the giants didn't spread the flame in a swarm like the little ones had to... my eyes darted to the bucket Leland hauled.

Focus. Saizsir closed on us — one leg limp as Yasha's toxin took effect, causing a stumble in his gait. One I took full advantage of — shrinking range quickly before he could bring his size to bear.

I dashed in beneath a clumsy strike — doubted his prey ever came at him — and ducked the paralyzed leg as it swung uselessly beneath him, aiming for the one he'd planted to take a swing at me.

CRACK. Satisfaction as the knuckle buster drove the strike home — right at the joint. Chef's kiss.

The sapphire giant's leg folded in a spray of purple. Two legs down, he'd be hurting — barely mobile. His song had gone quiet in the melee — no witty repartee, thank goodness — but still present. He wasn't dead yet.

Time to fix that.

I leapt, grabbing the crippled leg and launched myself up to scrabble for his back. I've never ridden a bucking bull before — Olly was the farm boy, not me — but I have ridden in the bed of a pickup doing ninety through a rocky desert — and I bet this was something like both put together. Each of those was a much smoother ride than this wounded spider hellbent on scraping me off.

I punched. Again and again, I punched. The knuckle buster fired each time, but the blue armor was fucking thick. Every time I struck, the spider shrieked and shuddered, redoubling his frenzy, but I never punched through. Must've hit a nerve cluster with one, though, as he suddenly stopped bucking.

"About time, fucker." I risked rising to get a better angle for a finisher.

"KEL!" Olly hollered and turned the doom tube on me. "DOWN!"

The fuck?

No further word; he unleashed hell in torrents of steely death as I flattened to Saizsir's back.

I felt it then; hot viscera splattered down on my back, followed by bits of translucent wing sliding off the spider's back as Olly cut the wasps from the air.

The Avispa had fully breached.

I rolled off the stunned and stilled spider — he had bigger fish to fry right now, if he was alive — and I needed to get the hell under cover. Also, thankfully, provided by the big blue.

I peeked out to see the swarm fill the air, dive-bombing the big spiders, stabbing with their stingers. Damn overgrown murder hornets.

The Avispa hadn't started paying attention to us yet, thank goodness. I saw Doc and Leland duck under a rock. Luna grabbed Olly's dumb ass and pulled him behind a boulder — my fault, really. Lost situational awareness in my personal grudge, and he'd covered my ass.

Another wave came at Saizsir, jabbing into the gemstone armor — more effectively than my knuckle busters. My cover thrashed in pain as their hypodermic asses penetrated carapace — guess he was only mostly dead. Pity.

I dashed for the boulder next to Luna and Olly. Wasn't much cover from above, but we were on the opposite side from the kamikaze wasps. Plus, we'd at least have our backs to something.

"What now?" Besides breathe while Saizsir's posse took their beating.

Luna'd pulled his knife — matte black blade, paracord handle. Standard except for the dead letters etched into the steel — same as his tiles. I'd never seen him use it — on anything — but I imagine the sapper's blade was wicked.

Quickly proven as one of their stabby asses landed too close — perching on the boulder above Luna's head.

KSST SSKT the blade sliced the bug to bits — cutting further than the short knife should, but all that mattered was the threat was neutralized.

"Nice knife," I approved. As pieces of dead wasp littered the ground.

"Sometimes a sharp knife's all you need," the sapper smiled. "Or C4."

"Amen," Olly echoed. Growing up on a farm, I'm sure the big man knew his way around a knife. He spun, launching a barrage from the twelve-phase at two more coming in from our six.

Dust kicked up as they slammed to the ground, their wings clipped. One struggled, annoyingly un-splatted. Ciacha took care of that, appearing suddenly in the rising dust to squash the grounded wasp.

"We must flee," Olly translated as Ciacha took up rear guard, webs strung between her front legs to snare dive-bombers.

"No shit." Doc, ever helpful.

The buzzing grew louder. I risked poking my head over cover to see exactly what we'd have to get through. Stupid mistake. The instant I even thought about raising my head, a stinger struck the rock — sending me back in a roll.

"Mother..." I sprawled under Ciacha as Luna field dressed the wasp in quick, criss-cross slices. The pieces looked a lot smaller when they weren't coming at my face — the bugs themselves were probably no bigger than a watermelon. Still too damn big — if I could just land a hit...

"The drones distract as the queen directs," Osiet with the cryptic message floating in the air. "Hunting and spreading her genes."

"Well, where's the damn queen then?" Talking to voices in my head. Normally, that'd land me in a padded cell, but out here, it was par for the course.

"They have queens? I thought bees had queens. Not wasps," Olly mused aloud, slightly distant as Lulu put on the Nature Channel for the big man.

"Science later," Luna interrupted. "How do we kill la reina?"

"Same as the others, I guess," I shrugged, flexing my eager hands. "Mash 'em, slice 'em..."

"Stick 'em in a stew?" Leland with the bad joke. "Nasty."

"Olly." I had an idea. "Shoot the fuckers when I say." It was a bad idea. "Doc, get ready to patch me up." Grim as I skirted the edge of the boulder. "And don't light the damn things on fire." I'd seen him thumbing his grenades, and the last thing I needed was flaming death-needles trying to stick my ass.

We all die sometime.

/15/

Between the blind man, the big man, the spook, and the doc, I was the fastest on my feet. Well, Doc might beat a throw to home, but that was in a straight line. So I ran.

I ran out of cover and into the waiting swarm, bobbing and weaving as the needles came. Way I figured it, the queen would be the one *not* attacking me. Process of elimination — hopefully before I was.

Thunder chuckled in my heart as I felt a manic burst of energy lighten my feet as I danced around the daggers streaking mid-air. One I punched, feeling only the breeze of wings before my buster could even trigger. I spun as another slammed into me from the side — stinger deflecting off my body armor — bringing an arm around for a backhand.

CRUNCH

No time for satisfaction as two dove in from opposite directions. Seemed I had their attention. I dodged and dove into a roll, kicking into a run as a third came at me from behind.

"That's it," I grinned, putting on speed. "Line on up. Where are you, queenie?"

Buzzing grew louder as my conga line closed in, more joining as I dodged their failed dive-bombs. I was getting used to their speed and agility, but my chest already felt like it would burst — still, I had to keep going. In through the nose, out through the mouth. Measured and even as darkness crept in at the edges. Just the way G had trained me.

Focus. Reminisce later.

I vaguely became aware of each of my pursuers, sensing their exact location and speed. Calculating the swarm as they trailed behind me. Faster and faster my legs pumped. Where was it?

One prick stuck me, glancing. Another caught up, too. Fuck it, time to clear the air.

"Ready!" I yelled, angling my path toward the squad's cover.

Olly popped up, twelve-phase humming. I veered left as the big man opened fire — steel flying a hairsbreadth from my face. Straight into the wasps with satisfying cracks and splats.

The swarm followed as I peeled off, scrambling away from the death flung their way. Olly adjusted fire, tracking the wasps trailing behind me. Half a dozen broke off, heading straight for him as he strafed the swarm.

Still he fired at the ones on my heels — splat by splat, their ranks quickly thinned as the solid metal chunks crunched into them — braving oncoming death.

Luna had him covered, slicing the stabby asses as they came close to the death dealer — their pieces twitching and wriggling as they fell from the air.

The whuffing stopped while the buzz did not. Then I heard the empty click of the doom tube as rounds ran out — with two bogeys still at my back.

"Hang on, Kel!" Olly yelled as I ran, looking for a spot to lose the pursuit. "Need some ammo here!" Strings of Spanish curses mixed with some from the dead tongue as Luna burst boulders for rounds.

"Runnin' out of road here!" I zagged into a zig, kicking off a rock wall to keep speed — flipping over one of the pursuing wasps. I tried for a punch, but whiffed — mostly suppressive. Would'a been nice to connect, but more important to keep it out of my face.

Not that it mattered when I fell on said face anyway — treacherous foot catching on a crack that sent me sprawling.

SPLAT SPLAT I felt hot viscera splash down my back as I went ass over tit.

Damn dude, cut that close, I didn't say aloud as I rolled to my feet, ready to punch another. None came. Thunder rumbled in my heart.

I'd been about to say as much when Luna screamed, rising into the air.

He'd found the queen — rather, it'd found him. The giant-fucking-whore. It'd stabbed him through the back, stinger coming out his stomach, a few of his guts with it. Bastard had grabbed hold of the stinger and went along for the ride.

"LUNA!"

I sprinted toward the sapper taking flight. Olly turned, raising the doom tube — no clean shot.

Helpless, we watched the queen carry our friend higher and higher. Olly kept a bead, ready to put Luna out of his misery — if the rounds could reach.

"There is nowhere yours cannot reach," Ros with the tempting words — motes then flowing upward.

Rider-sight kicked on — apparently useful in more than utter darkness — and I saw the glyphs streaming from Luna's hands around the stinger and up into the queen wasp that carried him. Dead tongue slithering over the overgrown bug's husk.

"Puta madre," he grimaced, knuckles and face going white. The binding words constricted, rupturing the queen's hard skin. It screeched and writhed mid-air, coming undone — unable to resist the sapper's spell.

The broken bits of queen — now contorted in pain — dropped away. She tried to shake Luna loose from her sting, but he held firm until its end, when the wings fluttered free.

He, too, fell — no longer defying gravity.

We ran. Hundred meters, two, I don't know how far the queen had gotten before Luna's Ginsu act sliced and diced the giant-ass bug — and I mean *giant*. The queen was a *lot* bigger than a watermelon. More like a water barrel.

"I got 'em," Doc yelled, waving us off. "I got 'em," with a sliding catch. Already treating the gut wound when Olly and I got there.

"Hang in there, amigo. Doc'll get you fixed up," Olly kneeled at his side. "Won't ya, Doc," his tone turned dark.

"Do what I can." Doc Lowry stuffed a wad of chaw in his cheek, working up a good spit. His hands examined the black stinger sticking out of Luna's gut. Barbed both ways, from what I could see through the blood. Sh it.

Worse, the barbs seemed to be biting deeper despite the severed queen.

"*Me cago en la madre que te pario pendejo de mierda,*" Luna's eyes rolled back from the pain.

"Queen's Revenge," Ros offered subtitled sympathy — words again flowing to show Luna's binding glyphs. This time pulsing glyphs of white intermingled the black bindings. Must have been the doc's healing.

Her royal fuckness herself had bounced, broken and torn, opposite from Luna's landing. Ciacha pounced, squeezing the stricken queen's head between her mandibles — gouging multifaceted eyes, crushing it with a satisfying POP.

Luna's lips moved, weakly muttering. I watched the bindings flow forth, settling around the wound — probably holding his insides in place. Doc spat some of the juice he'd been working on in the wound. It glowed blazing white in the rider-sight.

"Is that sanitary?" The big man hovered, second-guessing the doc. Lowry didn't respond, focused on his work and his chant.

"Olly," I pulled his attention from the triage. "C'mon, brother. Let the doc work." I put my hand on his arm. He shook it off.

"Bostock," Luna snapped through the pain. "Pull security," he groaned, resuming the weak chant — eyes squeezed shut against the pain, slipping into prayer. " *Padre santo que estas en los cielos...*"

"Doc's got him," I tried again. "Ciacha," I turned my attention to her. "Cover 'em up?"

No webs in sight, she chittered.

"Says okay," Olly didn't fully translate as the spider took up position over the medic and his patient.

As we swept out, I heard the doc conscript Leland's hands to hold bits of Luna together and, quote, "For god's sake, don't look at him."

From the mess I'd seen, might have been worth it to risk a peek — it'd fix him or end the suffering. See if Doc could work a miracle first.

Back to back — Olly swept the twelve-phase's tail over the rubble Luna'd made, refilling the railgun's hopper as we scanned for threats.

"Cut it close back there with the reload," I changed the subject — putting a little levity in my voice. "Thanks. Saved my bacon." I didn't know how close the bugs had been to stabbing me as I stumbled.

"What ya talking about, Kel? I was Winchester," Olly perplexed.

"You mean you didn't splat the last two?" I was confused, too. Rounds out?

"Not me, bro," Olly grimaced as I peeked over my shoulder. "I heard the turbo-props over my shoulder and saw Luna..." he trailed. "Thought you'd bought it, too." The big man shook his head to clear the pain.

Thunder laughed away in my heart. Had... later. The rocks rippled, heading toward us.

"Two o'clock low," I called the position. Olly and I swapped 'round so the doom tube could lock on the target.

The sites wavered as the illusion never resolved into form. My eyes tried to make sense of the bendy, limping rocks. Limping?

"Hold," I told the big man. "Might be a friendly." A web sprouted at our feet.

"My thanks," Yasha's song sang. The spy mistress hobbled closer — one leg missing to a stub. *"We must hurry. Another swarm comes."*

Peachy. Just peachy.

"Doc," I checked in. "Get him ready to load up. Company's coming."

Luna didn't look so good. Doc's face confirmed. The sapper'd stopped his chant, black binding glyphs fading, but still visible. It wasn't active, but he'd made it last — for a little bit.

"Damnit, Blaese, he'll die if we move him," Lowry complained.

"Make it so he doesn't," I ordered. "Or we're all in the fucked bucket," I nodded at Leland's charge. "Olly," I didn't really want to know, "how long on the clock?"

"Tweeeenty-three minutes," he relayed from Lulu, "and sixteen seconds."

Hoo-boy.

"Twelve," Olly counted.

"I get it." Four seconds of indecision. Ditch and run? Top speed, we could make it fifteen, twenty klicks before it blew. Could Ciacha? Probably not. Olly, me, Doc, maybe Leland? Luna... Scrap that.

"Ten," time slowed as I thought. "Nine. What's the plan, Kel?"

Same as before, I wanted to say. But the situation had changed.

"The weapon is still active?" Alarm filled her thread. Ciacha chittered in response.

"Snitch," Olly grumbled. "Told'er Luna's the one who could've shut it down."

"Leave! Leave now," Yasha played shrill. *"You endanger those sheltered below."*

Around us, I saw the air ripple — her spies closing for a strike?

"We will," I placated. "Help us with a sling for him, and we'll be on our way," I pointed to Luna. Safely wrapping the sapper up for transit was the least they could do. "Doc, Leland..."

Ciacha beat me to it, gently lifting Javier to her back, webbing him tight as she went — her nursing skills on display.

"Says she'll carry Luna," Olly translated. "Doc and Leland, too," he added as she offered a leg up.

"Fuck that, no way," Doc protested.

"Walked this far," Leland stood, leaning on his hammer haft with bloodied hands. "Be damned if I get carried out now."

"Fine," I didn't argue with Leland, his choice. "Just keep up." But the doc... "Get up there, Doc. You still gotta fix Luna."

Lowry barely suppressed his sour look, grumbling as he started the climb. "Rather eat a bullet."

A bullet — tickled my brain. The idea, not an actual...anyway.

"That's it!" Could it work? "Olly! You still got your emergency ration?" It was crazy. Totally batshit. But could it?

He puzzled a second before realization dawned, and he patted his chest. "You mean this?" He pulled out a single round.

"Javier can't bust the case open way he is," I laid it out. "Ask Lulu if that can. Enough for you to futz the wires up at least."

"I don't think so. It's pretty tough. Not enough..."

"Oomf?" I supplied his trailing thought. "At home, yeah, but here." Time and time again, they'd given us oomf-and-a-half above what we thought.

"Enough to take my damn hand off," Leland waved his stub, illustrating the point.

"Kel," Olly thought about it, "didn't they teach you *not* to shoot the nukes at Ranger school?"

"Will it work?" No, it wasn't the best idea in the world, but it was the best we had.

"Might do," Olly considered, listening to Lulu. "Risky, though. Need to think."

"Think as you run," Yasha pressed. We were no longer welcome in the camp. *"This way,"* she led through a narrow opening in the rock face I'd never have seen.

"Think as we run," I echoed, forming the plan. "Leland, mount up," I pointed to Ciacha, leg still waiting. No time for stragglers.

"Thank you," I laid a hand on the giant spider. She settled her charge gently on her back as the blind man hoisted himself up. "But what are you doing? You should stay with your brood."

"They are safe now. And I will keep them so." I felt a deep mix of emotions despite the simple statements. Righteous anger, regret and reluctance, hints of sadness — determination, though, that particular feeling laced throughout the rest.

Her business. Time to handle mine.

I wanted to put a few klicks between us and the refugees before we shot the nuke. Granted, I wanted to just put a few klicks between us and the nuke period, but with just twenty minutes to work with... even at our enhanced speed, not possible.

"Move out."

/16/

"Double time," I called as we left Yasha behind. The hobbled spy spider'd had a hell of a time leading us out of the encampment through the cracks and crevices unknown and unseen — unlikely to be attacked as well. We hadn't encountered any resistance since we'd ended the Avispa raid.

Needed to eat up ground — about five, ten klicks should be enough. The path out widened between the mountain tops — not quite flat, but not hilly either. Glassy stone filled in the valley like sand — shifting as we ran and just as grating.

"Hope this shit doesn't get in our skivvies," Olly risked a wry chuckle, paying for it as he breathed the glittery dirt.

Stars streaked across the broad green sky — not mine, I didn't think. Ros remained quiet. Rings split the world in half between mountains to the horizon — an ominous rainbow in monochrome.

Ten minutes passed in silence — no idle chatter, no jokes or complaints. Most importantly — no sounds of the enemy. Just our feet kicking up dust and rocks, scattering them to the wind. Damn dirt was like diamonds — chewed up our boots as we ran. Olly and I made sure to stagger as we ran — wasn't sure the balaclava would keep the shit out as we kicked it up when it could grind through soles.

Olly and I outpaced Ciacha and her charges — but only barely. For such a large spider, she could really haul thorax. Much faster than last time we'd walked — but starkly different circumstances. Lot easier to move when you weren't taking prisoners.

The valley widened where mountains wore away — mere fingers of stone ground by wind as they dared touch the sky. Rocks round and polished like marbles littered the ground — streaks forming around them as they refused passage to the wind now near deafening.

"Five left," Olly kept the clock — screaming into the blustering gale. Now or never.

I scanned for any sort of cover. I saw a fold in the land a few hundred meters to our right. Better than nothing.

Olly and I crested the small ridge, sliding down the leeward side where the howling stopped. The big man stripped the pack from his back, laying it out to operate.

"Lulu ready to work some magic?" It was our only shot. I took up position, pulling security as he worked.

"Gonna try," Olly grimaced. "He's been running me through it over and over the whole run." He stuck his tongue out as he pulled the cover, looking for a spot to wedge the bullet. The whole thing was blinking angry red — and getting faster by the second.

The trick was finding — or making — a spot big enough to tuck the brass under and *then* striking the pin to set off the charge. Without losing any fingers.

Preferably. Then he could pull the red wire — whatever disarmed the damn thing. It'd be a fine balance — the delicate application of force.

WHANG!

Or he could hit it with a rock.

That was one way to disarm a thermonuclear device, I guess. Perfectly reasonable.

WHANG CLANG he hit it twice more. Olly stuck his fingers in the dent he'd made, prying the plate up a little more before wedging the bullet in under the blinking bits.

"Now for the fun part," Olly muttered. Time was running out. "I know, I know." He was arguing with Lulu. Bullets didn't work like that, I guessed.

Olly picked up his trusty rock, aiming for the primer pin.

"Been a good run, brother." His eyes met mine for a second as he swung.

The light went solid red.

And went dark.

"Is it..." I relaxed too soon as the damn thing started belching steam.

"No," Olly said, confused. "Haven't done anything yet. Should'a had another thirty seconds."

"So..." *do we need to run?* The steam cleared, showing the dead pack. No red lights. No hum. No sign of it doing a damn thing.

It'd stopped before Olly'd even done something stupid.

"Your dumbass plan worked?" Doc, helpful and positive as always.

Ciacha picked her way down the treacherous slope, sending diamond shards scattering as she brought the rest of the squad.

"Seems like," I hedged.

"Didn't," Olly perplexed.

"We're still here, aren't we?" Leland seemed unsure. "Shitty afterlife if not."

"Went into shutdown," Olly cocked his head, distracted. Listening to Lulu. "Doused the core, vented the steam," he ran through the explanation. "Slow down," he bit his lip.

"'Cause you hit it?"

"Hit it?" Doc echoed.

"Yeah, with a rock." Ludacris as it was.

"The fuck? You shitting me, Blaese?" I'd seen it and still couldn't believe it.

"Nope. That rock right there," I pointed to the one still in Olly's grip. Damn plating was barely scratched to boot.

"A rock." Leland giggled at the absurdity. His screws were plenty loose already, but this was just too much. He kept cackling from the back of the giant spider.

"Not complaining," I settled it. "It didn't blow. Doesn't seem to be leaking."

It spurted steam once more to make a liar of me.

"Let's get the hell out of here," I suggested. We could make our way back to the transit and maybe get off this cursed rock.

Olly hoisted the dead nuke out of habit.

"Leave it," I stopped him. "Just in case." I didn't want the damn thing suddenly deciding it wanted to explode after all.

"But..." he struggled, his face torn.

"Leave it," I repeated. "Take the gun, leave the nuke." It was his pride and joy. "Isn't powering shit now anyway."

"Fine," he slung off the pack, working to disconnect the modified railgun from the repurposed power supply. I guess when you've hauled something through hell and back, you kinda get attached to it — even if it could, in fact, immolate you at any second.

"Not so fast, big man," a new voice said, appearing on the slope above. Jagged scree clattered beneath his feet, kicked — making a show of his presence. He wore a tattered mantle the color of burnt canyon rocks, broken up with bits of webbing over otherwise standard BDUs and kit. Goggles — *wish I had some* — and balaclava covered his face.

"Identify yourself!" If I'd had a gun, I'd have trained it on the newcomer. Same reflex had Olly point the dead doom tube. Might not work, but should be enough to give anyone pause.

Except this guy. He laughed and jumped down the slope. Where had I...

"Where's the fun in that?" He interrupted my thought and closed range quickly, sidestepping Olly and coming straight at me — footwork quick and nimble. I heard a buster charge — but not mine.

Shit.

I clenched, drawing my elbows in and closing my guard — bracing for one hell of an impact. Briefly, I caught glimpse of name tape as the mantle flared out behind the attacker drawing back to strike - Lima Charlie one-four. So the fucker *was* alive. I felt a breeze by my ear and a love tap to my liver. Followed by familiar laughter.

"Goddamn asshole," I swung a hook in earnest — aiming for a head I knew would be ducking by then. How many times had I seen that pattern. Next, he'd pop up for an upper like a damn video game character.

I snapped my head back as the buster scraped my chin and grabbed him for a hug.

"Kel!" Olly'd dropped the railgun and barreled toward us, ready to throw down. Ciacha chittered angrily, readying a web to sling.

"S'alright," I waved them off. "I know this fucker." I threw my arm over his shoulder.

"Is that any way to talk about your big brother, huh twerp?" Gerald pulled the face coverings off and shook his head — grit raining from his hair.

"You mean the one they told me was dead, but who's showing up on this forsaken rock looking to pick a fight?" I punched him playfully. "That big brother?" I spat out the dust that'd gotten into my mouth from Gerald's head shake.

"If they told you I was dead, what the hell are you doing here?"

"Avenging you, for one," I smart-mouthed. "Two, someone else told me you weren't. So I came looking."

"Well, that was dumb, but love you too, bro," he squeezed me.

"So's signing up with this death squad in the first place," I countered. "The fuck you doing volunteering for this shit?"

His face darkened before switching subjects. "You still leave your flank way too open," he punched at my kidney again. "Didn't I teach you better than that?"

"To totally interrupt this heartwarming reunion," Doc Lowry did, "shouldn't we be getting away from that nuke?"

"Who's the jackass?" Gerald ignored his question.

"Medic. What the hell are you doing here?" Back on topic.

"Cleaning up your mess is what," he broke the hug. "*And* saving your ass in the process, ungrateful prick. Who do you think flipped the off switch?" That explained it. "And…"

"*My* mess!?" I interrupted. "This whole mission was fucked from the start."

"Always are," he spat. "Taught you that, too. Do better."

He had. Couldn't really complain — shit was shit no matter how shitty shit was — just didn't like being called to task by my big brother.

"But more than you know," Gerald went on. "Luna's down?" He looked over at the sapper on the spider's back.

"Doc's working on it," I confirmed. "We were about to head for the transit, but I get the feeling you got something else in mind."

"Got it in one," Gerald smirked. "Your CO's gone rogue, and you get to handle it."

Payback's a bitch.

Part 4: Gravity's Hammer

/17/

Ames, rogue. That part didn't surprise me. The religious zealot had more than a few loose screws even *before* I dropped space rocks on him. That the cockroach had survived, though, kinda did.

"Precision aids in such matters," Ros offered the wisdom of the Eshali — thunderous tongue echoing strangely.

"What's with the freakshow grin?" Gerald squinted and rubbed his temple. He hadn't seen Ros' battle mania plastered on my face before.

"Does that now," Olly drawled. "Thank his rider. How'd you find us?"

"Creepy," he shook his head clear. "Wasn't hard, big man," Gerald patted the failed failsafe on Olly's back.

"Brass got twitchy when it didn't report - or blow - sent me to see why."

"Why you?" I wiped the grin from my face. Gerald was top-notch, sure... but something still didn't track.

"MOD," Luna groaned, joining us.

"Luna!" Olly overjoyed at seeing the little sapper alive and upright. Doc had one arm, Leland the other. "You good brother?"

Olly joined the trio beneath Ciacha, checking over the packed wound — the webbing red with blood. At least his guts weren't trying to dangle out the hole anymore.

"*Tranquilo, tranquilo. Todo bien,*" Luna warded the big man off with some stilted Spanish.

Grateful as I was Javier was still on the right side of the grass, I wasn't losing this thread — pinning my brother with a hard look.

"Men of Deeds," Gerald shrugged the look off. I'd never heard of that particular one before, but I knew their like. Pingers who stuck their noses in when things got real-real bad. And now my brother was one of them.

"That's where you've been? A three-letter agency." I'd read some stuff I wasn't supposed to — how they made the verdict stick — but hadn't gotten that part. The file I'd seen ended with G listed KIA.

"Things happened, yeah," he said. "And I *was* dead, technically. For a minute or two." *And after that?* I wanted to ask but held back.

Osiet rumbled quietly in the back of my mind, saying nothing I could see — instead, I felt stabbing pain in my gut.

"Where we taking a walk?" I changed the subject. G would talk when he felt like it. He'd probably said all he could right now. Classified bullshit or some such.

My brother squatted, drawing a dirt map with his finger. Four tall mountains with hills leading up to them, barrens, and spots for the transit camp, spider camp, and our current location. "Tower cut into this mountain," he jabbed a finger at the new objective, the rear-most mountain. "First, though, we need to link up with Alpha company here," he stabbed a new location on the other side of the mountain spine. "They drew QRF and posted up there while I came after your collectively ungrateful asses."

"Dios mio! Santa Madre Maria salvame de esos putos pendejos." I couldn't exactly understand the words, but the tone was enough to guess Luna didn't like those guys.

None of us ever trained together. Kept in separate cells off-mission — if we even came back. The fat fucks running this squad of the desperate, dying, and the damned preferred keeping us in the dark. Easier to control. Who'd trust a bunch of criminals?

"Why aren't we going through here?" Olly pointed at the curvy bit through the hills and into range. Closer route, if rockier. Should have cover.

"You part goat, Bostock? No? Never make it," Gerald shook his head. "Steep terrain — nearly vertical open rock face. Enemy fliers'd pick us off on the ascent. Have to go the long way round."

"But it looks totally open," I scanned. "No cover. Wouldn't they just kamikaze us again?"

"Funny you should say that," Gerald grinned as a gust of wind scattered diamond dust over the sheltering hill. "That's exactly what we want."

***

A sun that wasn't mine slowly sank between the fingers of rock reaching for the stars in the alien sky as we braved the winds carving into our faces as much as the landscape.

Stuck here for another cycle of dark. Fantastic. My face burned, red and raw. I felt blood pooling around my eyes much like I saw in Olly's — his shot through with crimson. Looking all the demon I knew he could be in a fight.

A lone rock stuck up defiantly against the hellish gale that never ceased. Gerald motioned for it as we slogged forward, bleeding from a thousand pinpricks.

My brother had no such issue, I discovered as he called for a halt on the leeward side — the only shelter for... well, I couldn't see shit, so I wasn't sure how far. *Should see Doc about that.* And check on the spider-riders while I was at it.

"You need not suffer such stings yourself," Ros offered in the Eshali way — coy, guarded. Offering a bargain you'd like to not refuse. Olly'd said Lulu called their kind angels and demons in the minds of man. Aliens. Genies. Ghosts and geists. Got me wondering if they were behind the legends of fairies, too, with their bargains and prices.

"Doc, think you could keep us from leaking like sieves?" I grabbed some of the fresher webbing Ciacha'd layered around them, staunching the bleeders. She'd been smart, covering her backside with webs, weaving a low cocoon for her charges as well. Sticky kept the sand from digging into her carapace, but it was weighing her down as it caught the blowing grit — creating a diamond shell over her own skin.

Doc spat chaw juice in my eye.

"Nasty," Luna icked.

"Be healed," the medic grumbled, "and leave me alone. Got enough keeping him in one piece," he nodded at Luna. His earlier stubbornness had undone a bit of the doc's work.

"Sorry I asked." Disgusted, I wiped the brown spit away. Damned if it didn't work, though. My eyes no longer burned, and the blood had stopped dripping — only the nasty crap. "You good, Javier?"

"Never better," he grinned, one hand still to his stomach. I flickered on the rider-sight to see the bindings he'd woven over his stomach. Dude was tough. I saw Doc Lowry's workings too — dinged kinda yellow to the sight, now. No longer a warm white. Sickly looking where they pulled the damage and toxins away. Gut wounds are the worst.

"Keep fixing him, Doc," I glanced toward the sapper.

He didn't break his new chant but shot me an exasperated look. He was doing what he could. The yellow glow warmed back to white for a moment, dark black veins leaching from the wound into it.

"Leland," I nodded toward the blind man. Wasn't thinking.

"Blaese." He still didn't like me. Thousand-yard stare on full blast. I mean, I knew he was blind, but he didn't even look toward my voice.

"Lemme ask you," I stalled before going out into the blast, "that your first or last name?" The man didn't wear a name tape — lot of us didn't. For reasons. Hell,

I didn't even wear our unit badge — we'd just been calling him Leland since he'd hitched up.

"Last." Still with the cold shoulder. He sat on the fucked bucket, back against the cocoon — hooking into the strap-like webbing. Nonchalant — as if this were a routine ride before a jump.

"For God's sake, *Bertram*," Doc Lowry cut in, "quit being a petulant ass and be civil to Blaese. He and Bostock saved your ass from bleedin' out if you don't remember. Only ones who gave enough of a damn to."

Leland mumbled something that might have been a 'sorry' under his breath as he actually turned to look at me. Progress.

"Good talk," I saw myself out.

***

"All I'm saying," Olly was off on a tangent, "is Rob Zombie looks like the ghost of Randy Savage."

"Oh yeah," Gerald played along. "Everything good up there?"

"Touch and go," if I was honest. "But Javier's tough. He'll come through."

"Damn right," Olly nodded.

"Always has." G was familiar with our sapper, it seemed. "Good," a little distant. "We'll need him."

"For what?" I was curious. Sappers didn't get attached to units just to lay boobie-traps — that was just a bonus.

"You'll see," Gerald got cryptic. "Now let's get…"

Before he could even say 'dangerous,' it struck.

The howling wind and pelting dust had hidden the telltale hiss of the necrobot, leaping from the pit now opening beneath our feet. A new sound added to the fray as the spider's mandibles widened with a belch of fire.

I rolled backward into a crouch, shielding my face with a raised arm as flaming goo spread everywhere. I saw Gerald leap away from the all-natural napalm, mantle flapping in the scouring wind as flames licked the hem. Metal glinted beneath the fabric, and I saw him uncoil something.

Ciacha stomped at the attacker as the little firebug scuttled from the loose dirt toward Olly. Smaller than the rest I'd seen, this bot was coal black and greasy — shimmering slick from bits of glassy stone stuck to its husk sparkling in the burning light. Hadn't seen its kind before.

Its abdomen swelled sickly green, growing translucent as the membrane stretched thin as it seemed to suck in air. Readying another flamethrower from the looks of it.

Bigger target to hit. I shook the grit from my busters and charged the bolts, readying to close the distance and strike. With Olly's doom tube out of the equation, was going to be up close and personal from here on. Muscles tensed, my calves burned, eager to sprint into pummeling range. I lunged.

Rather, I tried to as my footing gave way in a gout of grit — taking a face full of it as I fell forward. Briefly, I caught a glance of something snaking up to my brother's hand as he twisted mid-air and sent it back out again — straight at the flame-spewer's head.

Snap. Crackle. Pop. All at once as the bot went down, deflating in a stinking pool.

"Aim for their heads, little bro," Gerald landed beside me. "Otherwise, they go boom."

Great. That wasn't in the manual.

"Headshots. Roger," I confirmed as I got back to back with my brother. The bots rarely operated alone. I scanned the ground for more to burst out any second,

"Maybe that was a straggler," Olly offered, seeing no further attack.

"Might be," Gerald relaxed a fraction — head still on a swivel.

"What was that thing?"

"Tick-tick boom," Olly offered, chuckling to himself.

I mean, it made sense, but my brother and I still raised the same eyebrow at the big man. He ignored it.

"What'cha got there?" Olly pointed at the looped coil in Gerald's hand. One end loose, the other hooked to a weight and a flag.

"Looks like a gravity hammer. That what tripped me up?" I shifted my eyebrow to G.

"Would you rather I'd hit you with it?" He twirled it in my face. "Should have, running in all hotheaded fool."

"He's got you there, Kel," Olly redoubled his chuckle — still amused by his naming pun. "Should make me one of those," Olly's gears started turning.

"Guess I'm simple," I shrugged. "I see something trying to kill me, I hit it."

"Usually a good policy," Gerald agreed.

"Hate to interrupt, ladies," Doc poked his head out of the cocoon, "but we need to...what the fuck is that?"

I couldn't help it. I bust out laughing.

/18/

The wind howled and scoured us less as night fell, and the stars surely shone beyond the occluding veil of jagged dirt kicked up in an alien haboob — not that we could see them. Or our hands in front of our faces. Or the ends of our eyelashes.

Conversely, it worked as Gerald had said — hiding us from the eyes of the Avispa. Since the little tick-tick boom incident, we hadn't encountered anything alive — or re-alived — as we trudged through the barren wastes of the badlands.

And even if they could *see* us, I doubt they'd have been able to do a damn thing about it. Nothing with wings was getting off the ground in that mess — even things that had no right to be flying in the first place. Like wasps. How the hell did any of that even work?

Maybe Loudain had an answer for that. He was smart. I'd ask Olly later if I really wanted to know.

Gerald's clenched fist raised, freezing us in place where we stood. Something was up ahead.

Rider-sight had been all but useless in the maelstrom — looking just like static.

"The vast number of targets clutters the eye," Ros texted by way of explanation. That, too, was nearly lost in the swirling motes I'd come to know. "Well beyond your comprehension." Rude.

The debris thinned a bit, falling from the air in which it'd swirled moments ago. I felt a funny feeling in the pit of my stomach followed by a strange dissonance in the thunder of my heart — now distant.

Bodies. Strewn across the crunching dunes. At my feet, I saw a single gloved hand rising up — unmoving. I knelt to take hold, but the whole arm came loose, torn off below the shoulder.

Another for the bucket.

It was definitely one of our guys. The arm still had our unit badge on the ragged sleeve — a blind Lady Justice. Sword held high, ready for a strike, and, instead of scales, a noose.

We were all fucked.

The question was, what did these guys in, and were there any survivors — on either side.

I wasn't seeing any hulking remnant husks where Alpha boys took out any necrobots. That wasn't good. If the wind hadn't even covered up the arm yet, it definitely couldn't have concealed something that size.

I took the arm by the hand and carefully moved forward, closing with Olly and Gerald.

Olly had fashioned his own gravity hammer after he'd seen my brother's — getting a tensile steel strength strand of web from Ciacha and having her stick it good to a big ass rock. Boulder, really. Size of a spare tire. His makeshift weapon now spun lazily in a close grip — ready to sling any second. Eyes alert for attack.

"I count six," Gerald was saying.

"Seven," I added the hand I held.

"Seven," he nodded. "Two teams," he looked at the arm, "and change. Not the full company."

"Spiders didn't get 'em all then," Olly smiled warmly. Never change, Olly.

Gerald knelt by a body, checking tags. "I don't think this was necrobots," he put his finger through a hole in the uniform.

"Too small for a necrobot," I agreed.

"Avispa?" Olly grimaced, looking up for an air raid. I shared a look with Gerald. He and I knew the winged menace couldn't have attacked through the blasting sands.

I didn't say it, but I recognized what probably made it. Silver-dollar size, just over the collarbone and into the throat. It was a bolt hole from one of the bolt bows.

This was Ames' doing.

"He's gone mad," I said.

"Told you." Gerald looked grim. The others joined us. Ciacha pulled security as Olly started policing bodies. Doc checked for any flickers of life among the dead.

"Wasn't a far trip," Luna said, leaning on Leland as they came up. "Major's always been un poco loco."

"Got that right," the blind man spat.

"Ames is one thing." I watched the bodies being gathered. "But the rest?" Hard to believe even those assholes would turn on their own like *this*. Olly stumbled back as a leg pulled off a man buried in the grit — it'd barely been attached, it seemed.

"We couldn't save them," Leland's voice broke, verging on tears. "Major took control." What the hell had happened at the camp?

"He desecrates the dead." Letters red as rage conveyed Osiet's thoughts on the matter — dead tongue stilted and curt, the thunder delving deep.

"Just got up like nothing was wrong. Like the spiders hadn't been gnawing on 'em. Like they hadn't had a whole ass sky fall on them," he turned his blinded gaze on me. I felt the daggers. The heat. And saw the burning red sigils singe the bandages. "All while Major was spouting some Bible verses."

"Man of God, my ass," I sneered.

"Quoting the Holy Scripture does not make one a Godly man. Actions do." A small prayer silently slid across Luna's lips as he made the sign of the cross. "In that, you are more Godly than that blasphemer, Blaese."

Leland scoffed. I stayed silent. Not adding fuel to that fire.

"His rider defies covenants and breaks the bonds of life and death," Gerald explained — words feeling oddly familiar. More eloquent than I was used to hearing from my brother. Maybe he was parroting his rider — whoever that was.

We all knew by that point the riders could control our actions — overriding our will —but now they'd apparently bought the extended service contract. Fine print bites your ass every damn time.

"Well," I stuffed that trauma in a sack for another day, "let's find A-co and go get our boys."

***

Easier said than done, as always.

Doc found no use for his talents among the remains. Nine dead, we figured. A whole squad's worth. Olly and I laid 'em out while Luna said some words. Leland stared on in seething silence. He'd protested as Ciacha wrapped them in webbing, but was overridden — no body bags, and we were out of buckets.

Gerald pulled security as we did right by the dead.

Carefully, Ciacha tucked our fallen under the hardened plates of grit that'd formed a sort of armor. Not all of them had been from Alpha company. A couple had belonged to our own — at least, so we thought. They were in so many pieces it was hard to tell.

We made a damn strange caravan as the badlands transitioned more to scattered rocks and scree littering the backside of the mountains. Two Rangers, a giant, a blind man with a bucket, and a spider ridden by a doctor and his cranky (im)patient.

"I can walk," Luna complained atop Ciacha.

"Normally, I'd say walk it off," Doc shoved some more chaw in his cheek, "but it'd do you more harm than good. Pass me another."

The pair were making esoteric IEDs for any necrobot spiders we encountered — something the equivalent of sticky bombs. Luna scratched some tiles with dead letters meant to bring down mountainsides, and Doc stuck a wad of Ciacha's webbing with a tail to sling it by.

We all make do in a pinch.

"Getting the hang of it, Bostock," Gerald approved. Olly'd been practicing his meteor hammer — adding another boulder to the other end of the tensile strand. It didn't have the same reach as my brother's 'shooting star' — as he called it — but with the grips at both ends, Olly could do his Kali shit and still crack a few carapaces along the way. Just like the rocks, his practice throws smashed. "Try using your elbow on the retrieval to add momentum for your next throw."

No shiny new weapon for me. Gerald just told me to focus on a spiky black rock he'd put in my hand without looking at it. Made no sense at all — in fact, I just figured he was fucking with me — but I gripped the jagged shrapnel of volcanic glass like I would a racquetball, training grip strength as I scanned for threats.

I felt a strange pull from it, running to my other hand. On a whim, I tossed it between my palms, following the arc with my mind rather than my eyes.

"Not bad, Kel," Gerald broke my concentration. "Pretty soon, you'll be juggling. Hey," he turned to Olly. "Tell your spider-friend to hold back a minute. A-co probably has some itchy triggers."

Couldn't blame them. I remembered my first reaction to our friendly neighborhood spider-bus — she still had the scar from it on her undercarriage.

"She can understand you," Olly said as Ciacha slowed. "We close?"

Gerald reached for his radio to make contact. "Half a klick or so," he guessed.

Wrong.

/19/

WHUFF A railgun round cracked against Ciacha's diamond grit armor hard, staggering the giant spider as another landed, sending sparks flying as it struck.

"Alpha Primary, this is Delta one-four. Cease fire, cease fire," Gerald yelled into his radio. "Friendlies in the AO. Repeat: Friendlies in the area of operations. Do you copy?"

Ciacha dove to the side, digging into the scree slope for more cover. She was the biggest target — doubt they'd even seen Luna and the doc riding on top.

"Bull. Shit," the radio crackled. "Charlie company's been compromised, *and* I can see that fuckin' *bot* with you fuckers. Fire at will," their CO ordered before cutting the squawk.

We scrabbled for the rocks as the rail gunners resumed their barrage. Strangely, their trajectories began appearing in my brain like Osiet Ros's orbital sniping solutions.

"You have but to open your mind," the Eshali tempted. Never again. I would not be responsible for more deaths in our battalion. The thunder sighed — for reasons I didn't understand.

"Damnit, Gaines," Gerald yelled over the incoming. "Stop shooting! We are not compromised, and that spider's a native asset currently carrying precious cargo."

Ground opened up around us as the rounds gouged deep.

"Don't think he wants to listen, G," I called over to him. "Any other ideas?"

No response as my brother leaned back against cover and slowly exhaled a long, cleansing breath.

Then the chanting began — so low at first I couldn't hear it over the steel tearing into the rocks, chewing away at our already scant cover.

I looked over to see my brother's face growing paler and paler as sweat beaded on his forehead. Drops collected in the wrinkles formed as he concentrated before rolling down his nose. The chanting rose, and the suppressive fire fell off. He stood, entranced, walking out into the bombardment.

"G!" I grabbed for my brother, missing as a round sizzled past. I snatched my hand out of its path — somehow sensing it at the last second. Thunder rumbled, well pleased, in my heart.

"What's he doing, Kel?" Olly peeked out to see what my idiot brother was up to.

"Hell if I know." Maybe he'd lost it, too. Seemed to be going around on this awful rock.

My brother's chanting grew loud and strong, invoking name after name in the dead tongue. Not that I recognized any among the litany *as* names, but I just felt they were. My stomach started feeling queasy as the chant overwhelmed the firepower, which cut off. Olly looked sick, too. Gerald raised his hand behind his head and motioned for us to follow.

"He's signaling us forward." I risked peeking over cover. Steel rain still fell cracking the ground, but slower — the bursts intermittent. I stepped out...

And jumped as a round landed at my feet. I made to dive back for cover, but Gerald motioned me to hold, chanting grown stern.

No more rounds came my way.

Next came Olly, and where he stood, no rounds fell.

Then Leland — a true test of faith for the blind man. But there he stood, hammer haft in one hand, bucket strapped over his shoulder. Straight and defiant in the face of death.

Lastly, Ciacha, with her charges, emerged from the scant cover she'd found. Her armor had taken a few more strikes but still held. After a remnant few rounds half-heartedly pinged off the plates, they slowed to a stop.

"You MOD bastard," Gaines came over the radio. "The fuck you do?"

A taut smile spread across my brother's pale face, blood dripping from his nose.

"That should do it," Gerald said, wiping at the nosebleed.

"Should do what?" Olly asked what I knew in my gut. He'd never felt it before, not like I had when the major had forced my hand. Made me...

"He whammied them," I had no doubt. My brother had done the same thing Ames had done to me and Leland.

"Not exactly," Ros weighed in — letters hesitant as they formed, slightly blurred. "Your major relies upon the order of divine ranks. Elzerath, his *rider*— as you call us, though it is an inelegant and feeble description — being high among us and due fealty of a host." That'd be our company's worth of riders, I assumed. "What your brother Gerald has done is beyond, now bonded with a greater being to whom whole hosts bow."

I detected a note of regret amongst the Eshali's scroll of words — pride as well, flickering at the edges. Along with - affection? I looked over at my brother with the rider-sight, hoping the letters Ros showed me would flow into some discernible shape to show me what Gerald had become. If even our riders took orders from him...

The firing had stopped for the most part — with the occasional exception as a few got shots off. Though none came close.

As we made our approach, I saw suspicion, anger, fear, and abject hatred etched on the faces of every soldier on the perimeter. Most brandished weapons they were unable to fire — the violence they wished to enact was plain to see.

I could relate. Last time someone fucked with my head like that, I allowed a primal force within me to take control — cataclysmically.

The violation ran deeper than controlling our movements; it bordered on...

"Do not your criminals wear chains to bind their actions?" Ros interrupted the thought train. "It is no different, in essence and practice."

I didn't like it, but my rider had a point.

"Ah, you *can* learn," the thunder laughed. Was that a joke?

A storm cloud approached in the form of Alpha company's commanding officer — Major Gaines. Heh, there's always one. Knew a Master Sergeant named Bates once — who came out swinging.

The punch aimed squarely at Gerald's jaw stopped an inch short. Veins popped at both temples, his face completely red.

"Major," Gerald saluted.

"*Captain*," Gaines spat — the loogie refusing to fly true as had the other projectiles launched our way, veering to the side of my brother's face. That he out-ranked my brother but was forced to do what he said by his rider no doubt ate at the major.

Gerald reached for his pocket and withdrew a sealed envelope, which he handed to the major. "Orders from General Phillips, sir."

Gains frowned, eyeing my brother as he ripped the papers open. He shuffled through the formalities and verifications, making sure the documents were authentic. The frown he wore slowly drew up into a smile as the major's eyes scanned over the orders.

"Alright, boys," he yelled to his men. "Command's given their blessing to hunt that traitor down. Like we weren't going to already."

One group cheered, another 'ooh-rah'ed, and more still rogered the order — reminding me that the Pandora Squads took from all the branches and ranks.

Enlisted, officers, and many from Special Forces. And they all wanted Ames dead. Couldn't blame them, really — the zealot just had that effect on everyone, it seemed.

"Alive, Major," Gerald emphasized. "He's to be brought before Command to answer for his treason."

"Be kinda hard there, Captain," Gaines locked eyes with my brother. "Last I saw, the bastard was already dead."

"Why're you so amped to go hunt a guy who's already dead?" Olly with the insight.

"Because he and what was left of Charlie company tried to kill us in our sleep," Gaines looked toward the big man gravely.

"Someone want to start at the beginning? 'Cause I'm sure as shit confused."

"Alpha company was tasked with QRF when your base got overwhelmed," Gerald filled in the gaps. "I'm guessing you got there after the rocks fell," my brother looked to the major for confirmation.

"Just dust and debris. FOB was empty, even of the dead," Gaines said. "Bunch of spiders, though. Husks littered all around. Put up one hell of a fight."

"After that, you looked for survivors?"

"Found them, too," Gaines nodded. "So we thought. Made our way to the secondary objective before the next transit opened for exfil…"

"And they killed the patrol squad," Gerald guessed. Bodies in the badlands. "Then took off into the storm?"

"Not before they tried it with a few more," Major Gaines confirmed. "Should have known something was off," he shook his head. "Fuckers didn't say a word."

"The Eshali may act, but we do not speak your tongues," Ros added in. Very helpful lately. Put me on edge, more than anything. The thunder laughed at my eternally amusing thoughts.

"How'd you know he's dead? They could have been in shock." Olly was still trying to make sense of the whole mess.

"Theliel told me," Gaines said. Guess that was his rider's name. "Called him an abomination."

"And they are," Osiet Ros echoed the sentiment of Major Gaines's rider. "Much as the enemy is." The parallels in strategy were apparent.

"We're gearing up to head out," Major Gaines changed the subject. "Have your squad grab a bite and resupply." He led us past the patrol perimeter. "Spider stays out here, though," he cocked his head back at Ciacha.

We made our way through the temporary camp slowly. Men checked their weapons. Shook sand out of their boots — what was left of them. The diamond grit was no less harsh on their feet than mine.

Olly bummed a granola bar off a guy. Split it between me and Leland, not having any himself. Luna stopped by a group he recognized — thought I saw another guy with a Sapper tab. Doc stayed with his patient.

"Got any spare bats?" I asked a guy by the name of Garner wearing just one buster. That was pretty standard since the knuckle buster was supposed to be an auxiliary weapon — I just happened to like them better than the hand axes and hammers and bow bolts most carried primary.

He took one look at my beat-up busters and tossed me a spare battery pack — only one, though. Guess I'd have to ask someone else. Mine were pretty drained from the shit over the last few cycles of dark. It'd been a long, adventurous walk for sure.

"Thanks." I clicked it into place, stowing the nearly drained one and moving down the line.

"Oh man, what an ass," I heard from a young kid. Good square jaw, jacked, too. "He was *the slowest* mofo ever doing his sets," he laughed.

"So what, Blake?" Another kid. What the hell had this lot done to get shunted here. "Like to take my time with a good pump myself," he ribbed the guy next to him.

"Serious guys," Blake, the other guy'd called him. "This guy, he'd do a set and pull out his phone and watch a video."

"I like checking my form, too," the one who'd been ribbed. "See if I'm doin' it proper." These guys were close, I could tell. Probably been through some shit together already. Maybe even before being carted off world.

"That wasn't what he was doing, jerkoff," Blake laughed. "He was watching whole-ass movies on YouTube!"

"No shit? Furreal?" The group started cackling.

"No lie," the kid smiled an empty smile. "I got tired of waiting, so I hit the dumbbells," he flexed.

"Dayum son," another squad mate sprang up. "Hey, hey y'all," he called out to us as we passed. "Let me introduce you to THE *baddest* mothafucka on this God-forsaken rock!"

"Oh yeah?" I grinned, taking the bait. My brother grabbed my arm, but I was always up to knock a braggart down a peg. "Why you say that?"

"'Cuz, man," Brown, by his name tape, threw his arm around his boy Blake. "This guy humped that big-ass railgun through that shitstorm and up this mountain," he paused. "All. By. Himself," he jumped at each word for emphasis. Blake, at least, had the decency to be embarrassed.

I suppressed a laugh. Olly'd been carrying his a whole lot longer and done a whole lot more with it than this kid. But that was too obvious.

"On top of squashing two of those fuckin' bugs. I *know* ain't none a y'all done *that*!"

That tore it. He just didn't know when to shut up.

"Nah, man," I smiled. I get building your squad up, but you don't tear others down in the process. "That guy," I pointed at the blind man holding the bucket, "I'd say *he's* the biggest, baddest, badass man on this spun-up rock."

They laughed and hooted at the apparent absurdity.

"That guy? The skinny blind one? No way."

"Ol' Bert there," I smiled harder, no humor in my eyes, "blind as he is — with one fucking hand, mind you — has hauled that bucket there, full of our dead brothers, up and down these mountains and through those scouring badlands," I paused for emphasis, "for the Last. Fucking. Week."

Mumbles flowed through the jumped-up kids.

"*And*," I went on, "he's still raring to burn it all to the fucking ground."

"Damn right," Leland agreed darkly, daring for any to dissent.

"Whoa," Brown started backpedaling, "whoa. Aight, aight. Then Blake's the *second* biggest badass out here." They resumed their traumatic laughter at that.

I let 'em have it, walking away.

"Must be SEALs," Gerald jibed under his breath. Of course SEALs would get put in A-co, the assholes.

Still just kids, I reminded myself.

/20/

"You know we're going to die today." A simple fact I considered as I stared up at the monolith rising into the clouds.

"Yeah, probably," Olly agreed.

"Let's get on with it." I cracked my neck, ready for the coming fight. The monolith itself wasn't what gave me the feeling of impending death — imposing as it was.

No, what did it was the sheer number of necrobots crawling all over the tower and the mountain paths leading up to it and the fact that the otherwise sleek and smooth stone of the monolith was pimpled with mud.

Nests.

"For new queens," Ros informed me, picking out each as a target in the rider-sight — I felt the meteors calling to me, begging to descend to their destiny. Drones tended each, carrying prey skewered on their stingers to each. The bodies struggled as they did.

Small spiders, most, but I saw a few four-limbed creatures amongst the eight.

I shot a glance over at Luna riding Ciacha's back — I shuddered at the thought of what might have happened had he not Ginsued that queen.

We'd moved silently among the rocks so far, concealed by the thickening fog. Smoke. Haze. Whatever it was. It stank like rotten eggs the further into it we went. I'd lost sight of A-co as we spread out, picking our way carefully up the scree-covered slopes until we came to a sheer cliff face.

Ciacha began to climb, attaching web strands as she went while Luna shored up the rock face. We waited at the base for the all-clear to ascend.

Movement left. A shadow in the fog — small and quick, dipping behind cover. Gerald silently slipped his weapon loose in his grip, slowly spinning it up. I readied my bolts. I signaled Olly to the near side of the boulder as I went around. My brother held back, ready to shoot the star either side.

A skittering sound followed by wild chittering came from Olly's side. I heard a thud and grunt from the big man, then sounds of a struggle. I raced around the back of the boulder, coming on his prone form as he fought off the eight legs smothering him.

Charging my bolts, I drove in hard with a left — missing as the spider leapt to the lip of rock above Olly.

"Kel, Kel, wait," Olly grabbed my hand. "It's Fred!"

The big man was all smiles as the dog-sized spider peered over the stone ledge — and if a spider could smile, Fred did. Happy as the little spider could be, he jumped down into Olly's arms.

At the worst possible time.

"Bostock, get down!" Gerald rounded the boulder, shooting star already taking flight as Fred was mid-fall.

Chaos.

Olly jumped for his little friend, grabbing the baby spider and rolling his back to take the impact of the oncoming hammer blow.

"No!" I lunged at the same time, trying to stop my brother — when the strangest feeling came over me.

Time slowed, as it does in those moments when pure adrenaline plays putty with it — stretching it and shaping it to whatever gets your ass out alive. Rider-sight kicked on, and I saw the hammer's trajectory — the path it would take, where it would strike, how it would rebound — all of it. And as I reached out, I felt the weight as if it were in my hand and *turned* its path — sending it sparking off the boulder Fred had jumped from as time snapped back into place.

"Well fuck me," Gerald looked at me, a stupid grin spreading on his face. "About damn time, bro." He came over and clapped me on the shoulder. "How long it take me to learn that?" He wasn't asking me.

Fred happily chittered, cradled in Olly's arms. "Young man, what will your mother say when she sees you here?" The big man laughed and gave the fuzzy carapace scratches.

I only half paid attention to them as Osiet Ros answered my brother in my head.

"You were ever the quick student, Gerald," the letters formed, giving me that strange echo once more. "Your brother, though…" the words trailed, and the thunder grew distant.

"Okay," I broke in, stunned. "Hold up. Wait a minute." I stared between the hovering letters and my brother's stupid face. "The fuck?"

Resonant thunder roared in my heart, flooding my senses and filling my brain with a tingle that threatened to shake me loose from coherence.

"Show him." My brother's voice faded away as I staggered against him — grasping for support in the drowning madness.

The world inverted again as it had that day now long ago in the not-forgotten white room — the day I'd opened the box.

Barren planet gave way to lush garden surrounding me — verdant purples and blues and yellows. A throaty rumble beckoned me toward cascading water — it sang as it flowed through metallic pans and pipes along rippling sheets of silver. A spiked fruit hung from the vine I brushed aside to get closer.

"Ow!" I snatched my hand back as the spines snagged at my skin, drawing blood. More spines grew and stabbed into my flesh.

"My garden thanks you for your offering," a husky voice said, gently taking the vampiric fruit in hand and removing the barbs from my skin. "May its coming bounty benefit us all."

My eyes traveled up and up again to whom the voice belonged — tall did her no justice. The woman — I thought — now binding my hand with a strip of silky fabric could only be described as statuesque. Shimmering black cascaded from broad shoulders, draping her powerful form in midnight picked with twinkling stars. Golden hair flowed down her neck, framing an ageless face. A crown of spiked gold spiraled upward atop her head.

Eyes of the infinite locked onto mine.

"Take care, Kellan Blaese," familiar thunder laughed. "For one so guarded, you bleed all too readily."

Osiet Ros was speaking, and I could understand the words.

"How…?" I was at a loss.

"I am as I have always been," my rider smiled, leading me deeper into the garden. "Though you've always chosen distance," graceful fingers flickered motes, weaving them into letters. "Subtitles? I think you called them. A buffer you created." The words she spoke even matched her lips shaded a lush green. This was Ros actually speaking — no subs, no dubs.

"Well, can you blame me?" I shrugged, cringing smaller in her overwhelming presence. "You just sorta barged in my head and started acting all high and mighty…and…"

"You feared me," she laughed, ever amused by my being. "Yes, so I have gathered," she pinned me with her gaze. "But I remind you I was invited, requested even."

"Requested?" I guess all that chanting I'd done had been the invitation, but never once had the name *Osiet Ros* crossed my tongue.

"Your brother, Gerald," she waved at a pool of still water along the garden path. The water turned red with blood. The blood of my brother as he lay dying on another forsaken rock he'd been cast to. Necrobots chewing on his bowels as familiar dead words called down oblivion from the skies. The same scene shown to me numerous times, from a different perspective.

He'd been the unit killer. I was legacy.

"You are the weapon they made," she countered my thought. "Limited by their beliefs and indoctrination."

"You mean the weapon my brother made," my face darkened. He'd requested Ros take me.

"He asked me to protect you," she defended Gerald. "Shield you from their full grasp as was he." Osiet Ros straightened, bringing her full, imposing height to bear. "Unlike the hosts, I am not directly beholden."

"Then what was all that 'By Elzerath's will' bullshit when you made me the major's apocalypse?" I could never forgive that violation.

"You are bound to me as I am bound to another from whom all flows," Ros spoke again in cryptics. "That act was at their behest, not directly Elzerath's, for a purpose unknown."

Silently, I digested the new information as Osiet Ros tended her plants — trying to place the pieces into some bigger picture. This Ros did not jive with the battle junkie I'd come to know, ready to cause an apocalypse on a whim.

"You still know me not," Ros sighed, caressing a pink bloom. "I am balance and revival," she said. "You think too much in dichotomy."

"The quick fam they gave me before shoving me through that transit the first time only went over the basic features and abject annihilation. The bounty thing was a side-note if we got stuck without food, so I could back up Bridges." Basically the same familiarization they gave anyone using a claymore — "This End Toward Enemy."

A pained look crossed my rider's face. Pitying my poor soul.

"They know only what they have read, not the true nature of death and resurrection. All must die to be reborn." The blossom she cradled shriveled and bore fruit, falling to seed and sprout. "Renewed."

All in the span of three breaths.

"You decide how and to what degree. A single stone, well placed, slays giants. A single fruit bore in the wastes saves a people." She plucked a prickly fruit from the sprouted vine mere moments grown.

I felt the untapped power offered in that fruit. The multitudes of what I could become.

I grasped the spiny fruit, piercing my skin.

"How we gonna do this?"

/21/

In an instant, I was back on the desolate mountain shrouded in cloying smog. Olly rollicked with Fred chittering happy like a puppy. Gerald held me by my shoulder as I finished taking the stumbling step.

"Welcome back," my brother said. How long was I...*there*?

"Our connection passes faster than thought," Ros's husky voice nibbled my ear, skipping the subtitles. "Your barriers have loosened."

"Barriers?" The question had been for Osiet Ros, but Gerald weighed in.

"That tracks," Gerald said. "You always turtle up," he mocked a kidney punch, illustrating my 'bad habits' again. "You're good at it — too good, sometimes."

"You can hear her?"

"A bit," my brother shrugged.

"Gerald retains our connection by choice out of love for you," Ros said. *That* was going to take some getting used to — the whole talking part. So close.

"You create a barrier around yourself. Close off. Tight guard, as your brother said," she critiqued. "You take everything on, take the hits, keep going. You let *no one* in."

"That's not true," I protested. "Gerald's in," I listed. "Olly," I thought.

"I forced myself in," Gerald counter-punched. "And Olly," he paused, looking at the big man playing with his puppy-spider, "who doesn't like Olly?"

"Open yourself to the wider world and embrace what you are capable of," Ros offered by way of wisdom. "You are more than the weapon they made you. Be the one you create."

"Contact right," we heard over Gerald's radio. I heard it, too, sounds of combat in the distance.

"Luna! Where's the rope?" my brother risked calling up through the thick white smoke. The boys in A-co were making enough noise to cover whatever he said.

"Paciencia, paciencia," the sapper called back. I heard him chanting through the fog.

"They don't have time for patience, mi amigo." Explosions cut with screams bounced down the cliffside.

"Here, here," he sent the spider strands down — the silks so thin I could barely grasp them. But they did stretch. I had an idea.

I grabbed the silks, wrapping them hand over elbow, stretching them even further. Time to do something stupid.

"Follow me!" I gripped the coils as tight as I could and ran the other way — jumping off the scree hill we'd just spent hours climbing. The web stretched even more before it pulled taut — launching me up the cliff face faster than I'd thought.

"This," Osiet Ros laughed with glee as I flew toward the battle above. "This is what I love about you, Kellan Blaese. Not the battles or violence, the sheer abandon with which you seek your goals. It is an exhilaration I've not felt in many cycles."

Atop the cliff, the smog cleared, and I saw chaos. Not only had Alpha company made contact right, but necrobots were moving on Luna and Ciacha's position as well. Something didn't look right with her — there was a hitch in her getup, as Olly would say. Had she been hurt climbing?

"You loco, hermano," Luna said as I landed, legs churning, kicking up dust.

"Never said I wasn't." I scanned the situation. Three black necrobots came in from the direction of the screams. "You good?" I asked Ciacha, placing my hand on her thorax to hear her response.

"I am well enough to fight." Her song was weak and halting, but there. *"Care more for your fellow war-makers. They fare not as well as you against the Songless."*

She wasn't wrong. Their whole company was in shambles — fighting in disparate groups.

The kid named Blake — second biggest badass on this rock — was frantically trying to get the railgun placed. To his credit, he *had* humped the damn thing up the mountain, and I saw two necrobots laying in death curls nearby, his axe covered in their blue hydraulics.

But it was futile. His loudmouth buddy — Brown, who carried the gun's power pack — got skewered by the stabby leg of the necrobot approaching Blake.

The poor kid screamed in fury, dropping the railgun and leaping with his axe swinging — burying it in the joint of another stabbing leg. Should have aimed for the head — the necrobot did, cutting Blake's clean off with its mandibles.

The rest of their company fared little better, I saw, as I turned my attention back to the three necrobots bearing down on us. Olly and my brother hadn't taken the fast way up like I had — guess they weren't as nuts — so me and Luna and Ciacha squared off.

"Got any of those sticky bombs to spare?"

"Used them making this foothold, my friend," Luna drew his knife.

I glanced at our feet. I hadn't noticed the dark blue as it seeped through the scree on the cliff top. Or the black bits chopped too fine to recognize as spider husk.

"Doc Lowrey and Leland have the rest." They were part of the rear element.

I wished Olly still had a working doom tube. Think. Luna wasn't up to running, but if they got close enough for him to use the knife, we were screwed anyway. Ciacha was holding the landing.

"Remember the stone." My rider-sight kicked on and targets appeared on the necrobots — and not orbital ones. Gerald's 'shooting star' suddenly made sense.

Too big. Too big. Not big enough. Aha. I found a good rock. Never underestimate the power of the perfect rock. It's a lesson we learned as kids, skipping stones across creeks, quickly forgotten as we grew up.

I took the perfectly formed rock and ran at the closing necrobot — familiar hiss loud and rhythmic. I dodged a stabbing leg, relying on my footwork as I spun, loosing the rock in an arc that swung it as if tethered like Gerald's hammer.

It hit.

Right between the dead spider's eyes, cracking the head open with a scream. The legs flailed, uncoordinated, as I slipped in for the finisher. Knuckle buster charged and ready, I punched — bolt driving home through the hydraulic trunk line.

On to the next. Two at once. Damn.

I felt drawn to two stones, one at my foot — the perfect one from before, fallen from its path — and another a few meters away, between me and the charging necrobots.

I dashed, pulling the perfect one up to my hand with Ros's bestowed power and kicked the other up as I passed, sending it flying while tethered to me by some invisible strand.

Juking left around a striding leg, I spun and let the stone in my hand fly on a long arc as before. The one I'd kicked came round the other side of the necrobot spider, picking up speed as it flew through the air to crack the joint of the leg stabbing at me.

I grabbed the leg as it went limp, hopping up to stare whatever controlled the dead spider straight in the eight eyes as I jabbed, putting the bolt right through the head.

The last spider lunged, jumping over the back of the re-dying necrobot to bulldoze me to the rubble I sent scattering. I tried to scrabble upright, then ducked, taking a knee instead as a prickling sensation at the back of my neck warned me of the steel weight that flew straight into — and through — the thorax of the spider as it reared for a strike.

"Good timing." I looked back at Gerald, just topping the cliff.

"Dumbass," Gerald scolded. "Flying off like that."

"They'd be dead if I hadn't," I hooked my thumb over at Luna and Ciacha — who seemed to be scolding both Fred and Olly, by the looks of things. I couldn't hear her song from where I stood, but it seemed stern. "A-co still needs..." I began to say 'our help' when the infernal buzzing started.

The Avispa had taken flight.

/22/

The swarm filled the air, soon followed by screams from the soldiers of Alpha company as the stabby asses found new homes in their hearts — bodies limp as they were taken aloft to the clay nests above.

There were too many. The clouds flowing down the mountain tower like waterfalls had hidden their true number — now blackening the green skies.

"Shit. What do we do?" I looked for some sort of cover, but there was none.

"Embrace the power, little brother," Gerald was grim. "Be the weapon you want to be," he echoed Osiet Ros's earlier sentiment. "Not the one they made."

I didn't want to be a weapon at all. I didn't want to bring down another apocalypse. I just wanted to do right by my brothers.

"Then bring down salvation," Ros thundered gently in my ear — warm as I'd ever heard the Eshali. "You decide how to wield it." I felt her now-gentle warmth embrace me.

I stared at the rings arcing through the sky above, barely visible through the swarm now, and made up my mind.

"I need your help," I looked to my brother. I was still new, and there were too many targets. I could nuke them all from orbit, as they were, but it wouldn't be precise — just more devastation. He'd done this before — I'd seen him in the memories Ros showed me. He had the skill needed to snipe so many targets from the a ir.

"You got it," he smiled.

"Javier, you might want to fortify," I called over to the sapper between Olly and Ciacha. All stared in horror at the coming doom. Grim determination was plastered on Olly's face. Luna was saying a prayer. Little Fred hid between his mother's sheltering legs.

Gerald drew a circle around us, whispering a few words as he closed it — his face seemed to dare any to cross it. I cleared my mind, letting Ros show me the munitions as my brother began picking out targets among the chaotic battle — if it could even be called that. Seemed more like a one-sided route. In unison, we began the chant.

Bits of space rock tumbled in my mind's eye, wandering carefree in endless circles above an even bigger space rock — until now, called to greater purpose. Gerald too, reached out, painting target after target — in the oncoming swarm, up on the tower, down on the ground as well. Careful not to come too near our brothers still fighting, still dying — granting a few kindnesses. Vaguely — as if from a great distance — I was aware of Luna building his shields around those in his care.

The chant grew, encompassing the entire cliffside as the target zone, then the entire planet. A great cycle of renewal had begun as I finally understood Osiet Ros's true purpose.

And the skies fell in streaks of white.

First, a bit of tungsten screamed through the Avispa flying nearest us, neatly sniping it from the air. Then, a clump of quartz burned down to the size of a quarter obliterated a mud-caked nest clinging to the targeted tower — the soldier inside grateful for release. Closely followed by a turkey-sized chunk of ice that lanced through the wings of a queen taking flight with a jet of steam.

On and on, pieces of the heavens rained down upon the damned. Exploding near targets from the boiled air within. Piercing hardened carapace with super-sonic speeds. Slicing and smashing, squishing the bugs against the tower as it scraped the edifice clean.

"Like rain cleansing the air," Osiet Ros observed. "Preparing the way for rebirth and renewal." The Eshali seemed well pleased to fulfill her purpose — clearing the dead to bring bounty.

It still didn't sit well with me.

I felt them fall. All of them. Every strike. Every death. Every bit of mercy granted to those I could not save. And with each, I cursed the ones who'd brought us to this forsaken planet. They would find their time so on.

But first, some accounts had come due.

Among the targets for mercy had been others I'd spared from more damage. I'd spied former squadmates from orbit — Lister, Ellis, what was left of the last Rossi twin. He was missing an arm — probably the one I'd found. He looked rough — they all did. I guess it was to be expected from corpses held together only by the will of a tyrant — and they couldn't rest until he was stopped.

I'd spotted the would-be dictator scuttling into a dark hole at the tower's base before I could snipe him — not unlike a cockroach — while Alpha company had been fighting the necrobots — leaving his brothers to their horrible fate. Hell, he'd probably provoked the Avispa's minions just to escape pursuit.

"You weren't satisfied with *one* apocalypse, Blaese? Had to go and do another?" Doc and Leland caught up with us.

"How many brothers you kill this time?" I didn't answer. Leland's bucket looked heavier now.

"*We* cleared the skies, swept the ground, and released those beyond saving," Gerald answered instead. He'd been the one to paint the targets, but I still pulled the trigger. "As I'd do for any brother facing fates beyond death," my brother stared down the blind man. "And wish had been offered me."

I glanced his direction. What happened after the cataclysm he'd caused?

Neither Ros nor Gerald answered my unspoken question — though I felt sure they'd heard.

"Did you take a space rock to the head? No?" Gerald added when neither Doc nor Leland spoke. "You're welcome. Saved your ungrateful asses." He walked off. I followed, leaving those two to cool off. Had to leave them here anyway.

"Ready for more?" I asked as we came to Luna's impromptu fort. Clever, really — Ciacha finally shed the armor she'd been hauling, and Olly piled a few more boulders for good measure while the sapper did his thing. The end result was a monumental stone spider protectively curling its legs. "Saw the major scuttling inside the tower."

"Roger," Olly grinned, hitching up his pack. He'd still been carrying the damn thing like Gerald told him all this time, just had the doom tube stowed for transport. He reached up to scritch Fred, who now rode on top of the hopper — much to Ciacha's apparent displeasure.

"By the grace of God," Luna agreed. The small man stretched his shoulders and cracked his neck as if he hadn't been deathly wounded — just sitting still too long and needed to work out the kinks.

"Those two coming?" Olly nodded, talking low under his breath. He'd seen the tense exchange.

"Can't," Gerald answered. "Both are a liability. Susceptible to being controlled by Ames through their riders."

"We're not? Howzat work then?" Olly was trying to add it up.

"Complicated," I grimaced. "Seems our riders aren't in his rider's command structure, technically. We were only there on attachment from weapons battalion," I said — the tactical and strategic options. "Gerald's... got something else going. And Luna?" I looked over at him to clarify.

"Teleth is not among the host of Elzerath," Luna confirmed — first time I'd heard his rider's name. Still didn't know what his deal was, but I'd guess he was an embedded spook.

"Thank you for your aid this far," I turned to Ciacha, laying a hand on our unusual ally. "I hope we stacked enough bodies of the Songless to satisfy your revenge and cut enough Avispa from the air to give your people a chance at freedom."

"You've done great things for my people who would have seen you fed to our young." Not a very comforting thought. *"But my fight is..."* she blinked as her song paused, *"...not yet over."*

/23/

"The hell is this place?"

Lights flickered on as we entered. Carved into the walls were glyphs of the dead tongue I'd seen in rider-sight tracing their way along — glowing as we passed. The illuminated writing chased itself down the meandering hallway, giving no clear lines of sight as the lights vanished around a curve.

"Old," Olly said. "Very old. Slow down," he grimaced. "Lulu says this was once Eshali. Their home?" Olly was confused by something Loudain no doubt didn't explain very well.

"A seat of our power, yes," Osiet Ros said beside me. "One of many." My rider appeared in plate armor this time — still dark as midnight with stars picked out against the depths of eternity, but no longer sensually flowing. Rather, exemplary of supple and lethal grace. "But not our home," she sighed, feeling to me like a memory out of place.

"The Avispa took it from them," Olly went on. "No, took it over when they left them..." he frowned. "Unattended? Is that right?"

"We had a momentary lapse of control dealing with issues elsewhere," Ros sniffed. "And an experiment went awry," she waved dismissively.

"Experiment!?" I rounded on the projection of my rider. "*You* caused all this?"

"They what now?" Luna hadn't been privy to the interchange.

"Population control," Olly scowled. "They made the bugs to fight the spiders. Lulu just admitted it."

"Pests in our gardens," Ros vanished.

"Mad." At a loss, I looked at Gerald. "They're all bloody mad." I looked back at Ciacha, turned around and covering our six — glad she wasn't hearing the derisive tone my rider used regarding her people. Her mobility was cut down in the tunnels, but she could damn well stop any trying to take us from behind.

"You expected sanity in war?" Gerald raised an eyebrow, motioning us forward.

"Guess I shouldn't, but damn, this is just extra." I checked the bend we came up to.

Blind curves sucked worse than corners — we had to keep zig-zagging every few meters to keep from getting caught with our pants down. Gerald and I took point, Olly just behind with Luna in the middle just ahead of Ciacha — the only one who could quickly squeeze past her in case we needed reinforcements.

A hundred meters this went on. Two.

"Those lights were already on," I signaled a freeze. "I don't think we triggered them," I whispered. The glyphs that had been racing ahead turned back at the lights in question, rebounding our direction until they vanished the way we'd come — running from something ahead.

We pressed forward toward the light, finding nothing. Another set and the glyphs did not return. A third set came into view, framing a dim opening off the side of the tunnel — the darkness was not complete, but it was close to.

A step closer and a hideous buzz filled the tunnel — reverberating off the graven walls. The pressure built until my heart nearly stopped.

"Steady men, keep the Lord in your heart," the major exhorted. "He shall strengthen our hands against this wicked foe."

Olly grabbed my shoulder as I nearly darted forward on impulse. Gerald, too, had put out an arm to bar my way.

The buzz came again, followed by a sick squelching sound and then a thud.

"Another sinner given his penance, by the Lord's grace."

"More bugs?" Olly mouthed.

"Deliver us from this evil, oh Lord," Ames prayed aloud. "We are Your instruments to wield."

More thuds. Squelches. Buzzing cut short by impact hammers, if I judged the sound of their nozzles right.

Behind us, Ciacha twitched, eager for revenge. She'd managed to turn herself forward in the narrow space, readying for the coming violence.

Gerald closed his eyes, focusing. "Ames, two with him, another down." He was quiet a moment before cussing.

I flicked on my rider-sight to see if I could see what my brother saw. I hadn't mastered it yet by any means, but I was picking up vague impressions. There *were* four people in the room beyond — larger, domed inside — three still standing. Dive-bombing them were some wasp drones — I couldn't tell how many — and a queen.

The royal pain hovered above the rest — out of reach of any weapon in the major's squad. It turned, multifaceted malevolent eyes stabbing in my direction. Great.

I quickly scanned further in. The motes grew vague and hazy — not attaching to any edges to highlight. But there was something... *focus. Need to deal with the queen first.*

Ciacha twitched again, nudging me forward in the close quarters, filling me with nervous static. Something was wrong. I turned to see what when it clicked. *Static.*

Her heart-rending song had ceased.

She'd turned Songless.

Eight eyes blinked unevenly at me as her head jerked.

"OUT!" I yelled as I ducked Ciacha's snapping mandibles, coming up swinging. I didn't slam a bolt home — should have, but this was a friend — hoping it'd snap her out of it.

"Once turned," Ros interjected, "there is no means to return."

I danced back, trying to distance myself — cut short as I slammed into a slab of Olly. Little Fred atop the hopper bristled, agitated.

"Kel? What's going on?" He hadn't heard Ciacha's song stop.

"She's gone Songless," I shouted, shoving the big man toward the exit. "Go, go," I called to Gerald and Javier. "She's not in control."

We spilled out the doorway into the battle beyond, much to Ames' glee, as a handful of drones assaulting the traitor and his men broke off to engage the new threat.

"You see?" Ames clasped his hands together, eyes toward heaven. "Divine providence smiles upon us! More sinners come for their deliverance."

The slimy bastard used the distraction to slip further in, his puppet soldiers closing ranks behind him. Luna tried to give chase, but the combination drone front — man and wasp — gave him pause.

The queen hovering above changed her flight, dipping lower and chittering loudly. Ciacha stumbled again coming through the door, eyes twitching — she was still fighting it, but the queen was taking control.

Gerald loosed a quick strike from his shooting star, aimed right for the queen. A drone intercepted the weight, body shattering. It was enough to deflect the attack and save its queen, though. Another drone swooped in to stab him in the back, only to be met with the star's return as Gerald pulled the line in around his elbow — ready to send it on another strike.

My brother — having the most range — focused on taking out the drones he could reach. Occasionally punching one of their hypodermic asses when they thought they'd be clever and attack as another drone died — perishing with them.

"Snap out of it!" Olly pushed Ciacha back with brute strength — slipping between her legs and holding on tight to her abdomen. "Fight it," he kept trying to snap her out of it — even as she pummeled his sides. Fred, full of dismay, chittered up a storm trying to get through to his mother. They were both losing ground.

I darted in as well, dodging her legs as they struck. One brushed my guard, and I felt the same song Nerix had sung when he turned — brief snatches and echoes of who she once was. Enough to know she knew...

Knew she was dying. Knew she'd been infected. Knew she was going to turn.

Why she fought so hard for her family's future as she felt the invader growing inside. Why she pushed even now to finish the terror of the Avispa once and for all.

I caught one of her stabbing legs in a clench — punching high at the joint. This time sending a charged bolt home, busting thick carapace. I felt more of her song — she didn't want Fred to see what she'd become.

"Olly," I yelled, "get Fred out of here." I'd respect her wishes.

"What are you doing?" His face went dark, grimacing as he took another hit to his side. Fred was still going wild with frenzy.

"It's what she wants, brother." I danced around another leg, charging my busters as I dashed to his side — needed to take out the leg that kept hitting him. The big man was tough, but too kind-hearted. He wasn't fighting back. Even though he could have snapped her in half, he took every bit of the punishment rather than hurt a friend. "I got this," I shoved at him.

"You sure there's nothing else." His eyes met mine, wincing as he took another hit.

"I don't like it any more than you," I cringed at the look on his face. "But it's gotta be done. Go!" I intercepted another strike, letting it slide past me and away from Olly.

He let go of Ciacha and grabbed firm hold of Fred as the little spider cried — driving forward and down, rolling under her to get through the door.

In a final act of defiance, Ciacha shot a glob of web after them, sealing the entrance shut. The queen above us screamed, flying even lower, landing on Ciacha's back and stabbing into the base of her head.

The spider went wild, bucking and rearing, trying to scrape the Avispa off her back. I rolled clear of the frenzy, coming up to meet her eyes as she went still.

I saw the last lingering light fade from those eyes as my spider friend vanished.

/24/

"No!!!!" Painful agony laced the scream that ripped from Olly's throat as he tore at the restraining web. Thankfully, he couldn't bust through.

I hated every second of it. I hated everything forcing my hand. It fucking sucked, but I did what needed doing.

I squared off with the empty husk of my friend as it rose up, the queen in full control — abdomen pulsing as it pumped more of whatever vile concoction they used to control the spiders into her system.

The Ciacha I knew and respected was fast. Formidable. A brown and orange blur right in your face - edge unseen at your throat.

The necrobot she'd become was a pale shadow of that deathly elegance. Made a mockery of her fatal grace.

It pissed me off even more.

I fought the tears back as I did what I had to do. Dashing in, slipping a sluggish strike and returning a double clutch bolt to the knee, rending it lame. I didn't stop.

I planted a foot on the curling joint and jumped for her back, and the wasp, foolishly lingering there, screamed as I kicked off a leg and swung at her royal hiney.

I barely missed as the Avispa took flight — grazing it enough to crack the carapace. It listed as its ass leaked, trying to fly higher up. I screamed after it.

The necrobot — I'd no longer call it Ciacha — rolled, trying to shake me loose. I tumbled off to the side, losing my footing. The dead husk pressed its advantage, coming out of the roll into a full bore charge, but it stumbled, two of eight legs crippled.

Olly was partway through the web at the door. Little Fred, too, worked at undoing his mother's last web. I needed to finish this.

I hopped back, trying to get out of sight of the door. She hadn't wanted Fred to see. I'd honor that best I could, but the tyke was tenaciously stubborn — like his mother.

The husk that was followed, leaking purple fluid as it hobbled along.

Calmly, I waited in a trance. All else faded behind me. I punched. Right hook. Duck. Upper, double clutch. It retreated, but I wouldn't let it. I pressed forward, slipping its too-slow strikes, climbing once more to that orange and brown back that was now so familiar. I caressed it gently, picking my spot.

And said goodbye to my friend.

The moment was too brief — they always are — as Gerald's gravity hammer grazed my ear. World closing back in around me, my senses caught up and I heard the buzz right behind me and the crack that sent it away.

"Get your head in the game, Kellan," he called, yanking the weight back to send at the swarming drones. "You aren't dead yet."

No. Others needed killing first.

"Fred, wait!" Olly yelled as the little spider ran for his mother's lifeless body. He'd slipped through the hole before Olly could get his big frame through, scurrying right into the path of danger.

The wounded queen dove for the baby, brown and orange like his mother, splattering him with the viscera leaking from her abdomen — looking to turn another to her cause. Oh hell no.

I leapt, catching hold of the diving queen mid-flight and pinning its wings to its side — crashing us both to the ground. It writhed and tried to stab me with the barbed stinger, but I punched. And I punched. And I punched until the heinous bug was no more. Not once using my busters — this was personal.

"You got it, Kel, you got it," Olly grabbed my shoulder. To the side, I could see Fred curling up with Ciacha's remains.

Around me, bits of bug rained from the air. Without the queen to coordinate the drones' attacks, Gerald made quick work of the scant few that remained — their killing frenzy abated.

"Merciful Lord *en los cielos*, forgive us for all that we've done" I heard Luna praying, "grant these poor souls your grace and deliver them the final rest they were denied."

"Amen," I added as we came up on the sapper praying over the cut-up bodies of the major's puppet soldiers. I hadn't seen him doing the work, but he'd been quick about it — his blades wicked sharp. I didn't look any closer, remembering what they'd done to armor-like carapaces.

"Ames?" Gerald scanned the bodies — only two, none of them him.

"Got away," Luna nodded. "That pendejo blasphemer scuttled off, leaving these two behind.

Lister and Ellis needed proper attention first," he made the sign of the cross over them.

"What's that zealot after in here anyway?" My eyes drifted toward my brother, looking for answers. "What's in here, G?"

"Power," Osiet Ros answered when my brother didn't. He shot her a look askance.

"What kind of power?"

Before either could answer, the cavernous dome high in the tower lit up crimson with a flare and an unearthly roar.

"Guess we're gonna find out."

Epilogue

What kind of fools run *toward* ominous red doom?

The same kind of fools who pin their hopes on what lies in a little box, now very far away.

Light years away from home, we fight the unspeakable horrors back into the endless night before they come knocking at the door.

We are the desperate, the dying, and the damned.

We are Pandora Squad — Wrath of Heaven, Wrought by Man. Says so right on the patch.

Also by

Felix Chance: Volume One
Second Chance: Felix Chance Volume Two

98 Rabbits: An Assemblage of Words

Web Serials on Kindle Vella
Felix Chance
Off Chance: Felix Chance Volume Three
Pandora Squad***
The True Tales of Elliot Shaw, Adventurer
Third Time's a Charm

Anthologies
"Into the Fire" in Hidden Villains Arise
"The Iron Sigh" in Behind the Shadows

My Thanks

Huge thanks to SGT Dave Waterhouse, 2nd Ranger Battalion, for his combat insight & military expertise. Couldn't have done this without you, brother. Hope your boys are good.

Thank you to Sean (miss you bro) and Eby for the feedback and motivation to see this through. To my brilliant friend who doesn't want to be named but helped engineer the doom tube and knuckle busters. Oh, and who also provided invaluable information regarding the various habits of spiders.

Thanks also to my editor, Kate Seger, and cover artist, Ben Mirabelli, for making the book look as good as it possibly can.

Pandora Squad is a dramatic departure from my usual fantastical fare and I'd like to thank everyone who's encouraged me to explore this new territory and also thank everyone who's come along for the ride.

Sign up

Want the latest and greatest on all of my wonderful words?

Just visit: www.halfacrepond.com/newsletter

About

J.E. Pittman dabbles in many speculative worlds. He blurs the borders between genre and crafts salient lies to tell a measure of truth. His work has been described as: capriciously chimeric, dreamlike, and a vivid enigma with indelible images stamped on your brain.

He independently publishes his darkly cozy urban fantasy series, Felix Chance, and his sci-fi action series Pandora Squad*** in addition to several web serials and anthologies. Discover more of his words on www.halfacrepond.com